To Sue,

I can Always count
on you and for that
I'm grateful. I miss
our daily talks but
only wish you Health &
Happiness & of course
a 'great read.....

Enjoy,

Vincent N. Scialo
3/15/06

Heigh-Ho

by

Vincent N. Scialo

THE NAMES IN THIS BOOK HAVE CHANGED TO PROTECT THE AUTHOR. THE CHARACTERS IN THIS BOOK ARE PLAYED BY. . . . .

Em Dee	....	Doc
Cranky	....	Grumpy
Dozzey	....	Sleepy
Merry	....	Happy
Yourshyness	....	Bashful
Hachew	....	Sneezy
TooDum	....	Dopey

AuthorHouse™
1663 Liberty Drive, Suite 200
Bloomington, IN 47403
www.authorhouse.com
Phone: 1-800-839-8640

AuthorHouse™ UK Ltd.
500 Avebury Boulevard
Central Milton Keynes, MK9 2BE
www.authorhouse.co.uk
Phone: 08001974150

This book is a work of fiction. People, places, events, and situations are the product of the author's imagination. Any resemblance to actual persons, living or dead, or historical events, is purely coincidental.

First published by AuthorHouse 2/27/2006

ISBN: 1-4259-1941-3 (sc)

Printed in the United States of America
Bloomington, Indiana

This book is printed on acid-free paper.

Dedication

As always, dreams can only come true with the people who matter the most in your life sharing them with you. So to keep it short, sweet and to the point, I acknowledge the following fellow dreamers. Excluding myself from the 'Scialo, Power of Four' I share my dreams with the ones who make it all possible.

Jennifer, my wife, my life, and most importantly my reality check on just what is and is not so meaningful in Life. I thank you abundantly.

Marissa, my daughter, who keeps me young at heart with her fine taste in music and fashion, plus quick on my feet for all the guys I'll being chasing away from her.

Jeff, my son, who should be cloned and sold to every parent who dreams of just what life could be like with a caring, compassionate son. Don't ever change. Charisma is a quality that will make you go far in life.

And as a special thanks to Kathy Zullo for her continued efforts in correcting my grammar and fine tuning my words to help the story move along. I was fortunate enough to cross paths with you and to gain a friend in doing so.

Also to Jennifer, my wife, for the art designs of the seven little men. Your artistic talents surpass all others I have ever known or come across.

And lastly to Jay Castronova for never saying NO to any of my special requests that always come with a deadline.

God Bless and Thanks.

Prologue

Perhaps at a quick glance, one might conclude that these seven individuals were considered midgets, but upon closer inspection one would determine that they were indeed men of smaller height. As each carried their pick at his side, the look of exhaustion was clearly evident on their faces. A full day at the diamond mine demanded the equivalent to a full week's worth of energy needed at other jobs in their past. But together working side by side, they were each in great company which they were not willing to give up. With their picks, which now weighed heavily on them, they whistled the tune together as one. A tune, which had never entered their minds until they each reached the region of the Black Forest so many years ago.

Delighted by what they had all become and fearful of what remained in their dreadful past. A heinous past none of them was ever willing to share. It was better for all of them to keep their past in the past. So in single file they marched as they whistled to their own familiar tune. A tune that for generations upon generations would be recognized by the simple start of the world famous phrase *'Heigh-Ho, Heigh-Ho, it's off to work we go'*...

1

"Come on and keep up! Yourshyness, would you please tap Toodum on the shoulder and get him back in line? That boy certainly likes to daydream and slow us up without even knowing he's doing it. We stayed later than usual and I would like to get back before nightfall," Cranky said as he looked up to the sky for reassurance that his last statement would be accurate.

"Would it really hunt, jeez, I mean hurt if we had to make our way back in the dark? After all, we carry these canteens, no I know they are lanterns, I take that back, just for that purpose," Emdee said as he turned around to glance at Cranky.

Cranky paid him no mind and in his usual unpleasant tone harped again to the others to hustle along the rest of the gang. Cranky was also used to Emdee fumbling his expressions and words. He saw the confusion Emdee had when he became tongue-tied and wished he would keep his words straight. He did this more often than not lately. At this time of day, twilight was not far behind. The forest was a second home to the dwarfs and all of them at one time or another spent many hours getting to know every nook and cranny of the woods. Their cabin was in a small clearing a little less than two miles from the diamond mine. The cottage was built of logs from the many trees that the seven of them had cut down with their own bare hands. The small cabin consisted of a large living space with an attached kitchen in the same room with a tiny staircase leading up to an alcove where their beds were lined up next to one another. Years ago, Emdee decided to label each of their beds and carved their names in wood on the footrest at the bottom of each. Many a night upon arriving home exhausted after a full day in the mines, some of them would call it a night and head straight to bed without supper. Complete exhaustion sometimes dulled their minds and confused by their surroundings, having the beds labeled with their names made it all the more possible for them to just crawl into bed without too much thought. Now as they headed in the early dusk of the evening, each of them stayed in single line. The cabin was just over the last hill they would have to cross. Emdee lead the way with the lantern extended out in front of him. He knew it was only minutes before they would arrive to the warmth of their beloved house. After just passing the well that supplied them with fresh water from the stream alongside the cabin, Emdee tilted his head down showing the care and seriousness that he always displayed to the others. How he himself became their leader always baffled him. He indeed was no wiser than Cranky and in certain areas lacked the swiftness that Cranky had in certain circumstances. The others, however, all came to him for guidance and support which he was always willing to share. He guessed that was why he came to be the chief of the group. Cranky accepted this and they remained friends no matter what situation they found themselves in.

Four years prior, they had all met in the diamond mine. Within a couple of hours at most, each one of them appeared at the opening to the tunnel leading into the mine. Emdee could close his eyes and vividly remember each of their faces as they approached the entrance. He was certain every one seemed to be hiding some secret. None of them wanted to divulge their own personal torment and Emdee never pressed the issue. Coming from seven surrounding towns, they all wound up in the Black Forest. It was like a magnetic pull for each of them with no means of stopping it or the force of energy that had them linked together forever. At first it took time for them all to become acquainted with each other and especially Toodum, who was speechless and found it hard to fit in with the bunch. Now they were like long-lost brothers who could never have imagined not knowing one another.

Emdee continued the last part of their journey home for the night. Close behind was Cranky followed by Hachew, Dozzey, Merry, Yourshyness and Toodum, otherwise known as The Seven Little Men.

2

"I'm so tired, Emdee. How much longer? Do you suppose we could perhaps stop for a nap?" asked Dozzey who was yawning with his arms stretched over his head as he followed.

"Seriously, you sometimes make me want to bust a gutter, I mean gut with the silly questions you ask. We should be home in no tea, I meant time. Hold out for a little larger, gosh I mean longer and count your blessings that you can be fast asleep quicker than the rest of us," Emdee smirked letting Dozzey know that no answer would be given to his question. Just as Dozzey was about to persist and ask for a second time, Hachew started what was bound to be his usual sneeze attack, which could last for minutes on end.

God Bless you's were heard from all but Toodum. Each one would say it in hopes that his fit of ha-choos would cease to exist knowing very well that they wouldn't until Hachew himself could make them stop.

The redness of his nose made the others glad that they weren't as unfortunate as he but also made them feel bad for him wishing they could help. Merry, who usually bounced in his gait, tried with endless effort to look serious and concerned but with his constant smile and never ending cheerfulness, it took all his energy to convince Hachew of his concern. Yourshyness, on the other hand, had to speak up just to make Hachew realize that he was truly interested in his well being as well.

"Hang in there kid, we're almost at our front floor, I mean door. Just a little while longer and we should ….," Emdee was cut off in mid-sentence by Cranky who finished it for him.

"Must you always confuse your words, Emdee. Honestly, it drives me nuts! And as for you Hachew, I thought you only had hay fever. Now everything you come across makes you sneeze. Doesn't your nose every dry up? Must be something in those two nostrils that catch hold of every germ that you inhale," Cranky stated in his usual firm voice.

"Stop picking on him. You know he can't help it. You would think by now that you would have adjusted like the rest of us have," Yourshyness blushed as he spoke.

"My goodness, we all seem to be on edge this evening. Perhaps a little folk dancing after dinner might lighten our moods. What'aya say fellows? Are we all in?" Merry asked in keeping with his usual bubbly disposition. Everyone agreed either with a simple yes or a nod of their heads. And as soon as they all agreed to an evening of song and dance, up ahead was their cottage with a fire in the hearth visible through the window. Emdee sped up and he was the first to notice that the front door was open. Each of the seven hesitated to go into the house. Cranky noticed that each of them was afraid and walked past Emdee and entered first. As the others, first apprehensive but now more trusting followed, they all stood staring and looking around the room. The entire floor and rooms were spotless. There wasn't a speck of dirt or dust to be found anywhere. This baffled them all and their expressions turned once again to panic. Cranky spoke first, "Now hold on here. I know we ain't never had this place looking so good. And lookie over by the fire. Somethin's cookin' that I know we never made."

"Maybe we should just turn around and leave before somebody jumps out at us," Yourshyness said, trembling as he spoke.

"And who would do something like fat, that? That, I mean that," Emdee stated as he stood still holding his lantern out in front of him.

"Well, I say we go on upstairs and see if the somebody may be up there. Who's in?" Cranky asked as he walked over to the cooking fire.

"On second thought, what if the legend of the Evil Witch mixed up a special brew and left it for us to drink and we fall victims to her spell," Hachew inquired trying to hold in a sneeze that was pointless. His sneeze startled the others.

"I say we forget about all this special witchcraft and call it a night instead. I'm just so darn tired," Dozzey said barely staying awake as he spoke. His eyes were drooping too as he tried to convince the others.

Emdee tried to comfort the others who now surrounded him in a circle as he said, "Let me be the first to say, there is no such person as an evil witch, queen or any other evilness. Do I make myself dear? Clear, you know I meant clear?"

They all shook their heads in agreement when Merry spoke, "Maybe someone nice decided to stop by since we never lock our front door and decided to come in to clean up for us. And what a pleasant surprise that they even cooked for us too!"

"Hold it right there, sunshine. Who in their right mind would have wandered off into the Black Forest and just happened to stumble upon OUR cottage? Think about it fellows.

ALL the way out here in the woods. Hopefully by themselves. And if that is the case, then where are they now," Cranky urged the others. They all just stood there staring at one another when Toodum stepped out of the circle and pointed with his oversized shirt to the stairs leading up to their beds. Since Toodum never spoke they all knew what he was getting at. He wanted them to check out the upstairs to see if the person might be hiding up there.

Cranky started to walk toward the steps leading upstairs as he looked back and said, "Enough of all this witch talk, lets say we all go on up these steps together and see if who or what or anything for that matter is up there. I say we band together as we have in the past and face this adversity if it is one head on. Are we brave or not?"

An echo of shouted out braves sounded off the walls and even Toodum who was speechless darted toward him first. As one, lined up in single file, they each made their way up the stairs to the top landing. Every one of their faces showed a look of concern as no one uttered a word as they climbed. When they all reached the top landing, Cranky was the first to move in closer to their beds. Emdee caught up to him and passed him as he held his finger up to his lips to silence the others. They all quietly tiptoed toward their own beds which were engraved with their names. The seven beds were all in a row. Emdee whispered out to them to stop before they got any closer to their beds and told them to go back and wait at the top of the stairs. Emdee would check his bed out first to make sure it was clear of any intruders. Emdee approached his first while the others stared on and it was at that very moment there in the quiet that Emdee had a flashback of his past.

A fearful past that he had pushed from his mind but now came flooding back.

Welby McWells

A little man who works miracles with tiny hands like a pea, So he shall be given the name of EMDEE..................

-Hiltrude

3

Long ago in a far away village, a baby of tiny proportions was born. Much to his parent's delight he was also a bit smaller than they had expected. The midwife that helped deliver him said that he would grow up to be a fine young man and put both their minds at ease although deep down, she too, wondered how a baby could be so small. The McWells named their baby boy, Welby after an old folklore that had been passed down from generation to generation. Little Welby never quite grew at the rate anyone in the village had anticipated. Welby was adored by all his relatives and friends in the town of Klackerstack. Klackerstack was one of many surrounding towns of the Black Forest that stretched for endless miles from hillsides to mountaintops in the region of Saltaire. The town itself was very quaint with three blocks of brick buildings and a road paved with cobblestones. The surrounding houses were in actuality farms that provided the sustenance of the small community. Welby and his parents lived in one of the brick buildings above a shoemaker's storefront. The three of them shared a one-bedroom apartment, which was more than adequate for their needs. Welby's father, Marcel, was the shoemaker himself. The building was owned by the Heron family, which owned most of the other buildings in town as well. Welby's mother, Marisol, was the schoolteacher for the village. As the only schoolteacher in town, Marisol never stood for any ridiculing or insults when it came to her only child and she was able to keep all the children disciplined when Welby didn't grow at the rate of his peers in class.

Her beloved, Welby. If by chance another child did make fun of her son, which over the course of the years had occurred, that student was punished sometimes more severely than he or she should have been. Recess was taken away and after school duties lasted much longer for them than any of the other students. Marisol would see to it that the classroom and blackboards were washed until one could see their reflection off the boards and floors. Most students knew the punishment bordered on a fine line of cruelty and shied away from offending her only son. As Welby grew into his formative years his parents both took notice of how creative he was when given a simple task using his hands. Marcel proudly told all the townspeople that he taught his son all his handiwork as Welby spent many hours in his father's shoe repair shop watching his papa in action. Marisol let her husband believe what he may, knowing all along that her son was gifted in his ability to work so lovingly with his hands due to his inability to grow in height like the others. As Welby progressed from infant to little boy his parents noticed he had difficulty seeing smaller objects and when taken to the village doctor two towns away was diagnosed with far-sightedness which could be remedied with a prescription for eyeglasses. So, as Welby grew at a much slower rate than normal, his body took on the look of a plump little boy and when added with glasses, he looked much older than his years. His speech also presented him with problems when he became a young teen and once again Marisol was right there at his side waiting to pounce on any individual who made any sly remark about his speech impediment. Welby had a heart of gold and meant no one any harm, but when it came time for him to verbalize on a subject he tended to mix up his words and this only caused him to become more confused. This frustrated Welby as he got older but his love for working with his hands made up for all his other discomforts. As a small child he first started helping the local animals belonging to his fellow townspeople. Welby could mend a bird's broken wing or a dog or cat's injury, too. As he grew to be a young adult in the village he had become admired by everyone in the community. No one, including his peers, made fun or ridiculed him any longer, which delighted both his parents. Marisol was able to walk through town with her head held high. Her son was fast becoming the local doctor in their village. Fewer and fewer people were leaving town to seek medical assistance of the doctor from two towns away.

He had proved himself capable of tending to everyone's medical needs. From a simple cold to a broken bone, Welby knew firsthand just how to take care of it. This amazed and astonished both his parents. His natural ability to teach himself about the human body and by years of examinations on animals when he was a small boy provided the experience he needed to learn more about the medical field. He taught himself about human anatomy and what little he didn't know his mother was able to acquire the medical books needed to help him teach himself. After many years, he was now established as the town doctor. His father helped him set up his practice down the street from his shoe repair shop in the old vacant blacksmith shop. Welby and his papa turned the old blacksmith shop into three tiny offices. One office was used to tend to the sick animals while the other office was used for the needs of the townspeople. The third office served as space for patient consultations for the various ailments the local townspeople came to discuss with him. No surgeries were performed in this office but all his visitors started here first before moving into one of the other examination rooms, as they later became known. Welby had a booming practice and this delighted him far more than words could describe, or at least he could say without mixing the words up. Patients learned to deal with his somewhat jumbled speech and with his general knowledge of all medical conditions accepted him despite his limited vocabulary. He was indeed an excellent doctor. What Welby didn't realize was how everything was about to change when he decided to perform plastic surgery, which he wasn't really comfortable with, on a local young woman who came to the village only a few months earlier. When asked of her whereabouts prior to coming to Klackerstack, Hiltrude would always change the topic. After so many futile attempts to find any little bit of information about her past and getting no response, most townspeople just gave up on inquiring any longer. After all, Hiltrude was not a beautiful girl by any means. Hiltrude was considered just the opposite.

Most people in town when referring to her said she was more homely then anything else.

Hiltrude was not too much taller than Welby and stood more hunched over than erect. Her straggly brown hair and deep brown eyes did her very little justice. Her nose was more of a bird's beak and her chin protruded more to a point than most others. If it weren't for the fact that she was younger than most other townswomen she could take on the look of a witch that most people had only seen in books. This disturbed Hiltrude very much. Witches were by far never considered attractive. Hiltrude knew she wasn't as attractive as many women she had come across in the village. Her main desire was to transform herself into what she always wanted to be; the most beautiful and fairest of them all. Hiltrude made her appointment with Welby one weekday afternoon. It was then that she tried to persuade Welby into making her the most startling young women in town.

"I just don't feel comfortable performing that type of procedure. I mean what happens if you don't spike,

I mean tike, no, like the outcome? I've never done this type of surgery before. You just whisked into town and now you come to me for something I've never done befact, oh there I go again, I mean before," Welby questioned staring into one of the most plain and borderline ugly faces he had ever seen.

"I was meant to be made beautiful. The fairest of them all! Don't you see? I have to be the most beautiful girl in the countryside. Any town I stop at shall bow to me when I pass. I was destined to be this. And you Welby, are the only one who could transform me. I've seen how you work on the others and there is no one in all of eternity I would rather have work on me. You must say yes to my request. You just have to!" Hiltrude pleaded as she sat across from Welby in his consultation office.

Welby was starting to get very uncomfortable, which nowadays took quite a lot to let happen, when he answered her in his calmest voice yet, "I understand your need to or should I say desire to be made beautiful. But I don't know if I can do this type of derk, oh here I go again, I mean work. What if it doesn't meet your desired results? What if I screw your face up?"

"You won't screw up my face. I know you won't. Please I beg of you. Please make me more desirable. I can't go on living like this! I NEED to be beautiful. When I look in a mirror I turn away in shame. I don't want to live the rest of my life like this. I WANT to be made special; better than the rest. The best of the rest. I want to marry a King who will treat me to all his royalties. Looking as I do this can never happen.

I know a King who will one day marry me if I can just look more beautiful. I was born to live the life of the rich and destined to be more wealthy than anyone could possibly dream of. Help me fulfill this desire too. Please Welby, PLEASE!"

Hiltrude once again pleaded now extended her hands across Welby's desk to take hold of his.

Welby pulled his now shaking one hand away from her grasp and said, "Let me think about this. I need a day or two before I can make my decision. Really, Hiltrude, let me stink, I mean think about miss, this. I mean this whole request. It really is too much for me to handle at one sitting with you. I will get back to you. Of that I promise. One way or another I will let you know my answer."

Hiltrude looked at Welby with the most saddened stare he had ever seen. Then as if nothing at all had taken place, her whole appearance changed. She stood up pushing her chair back as she did. Facing her worst fear, Hiltrude changed her mind and tried a new approach. Before she left his office she turned to him and in a very stern voice which he had never heard in the past said, "Two days, Welby. You have two days to decide in which case I know your answer will be yes. Of that I AM certain. You will perform the surgery and you WILL make me the most beautiful girl in this countryside. I really leave you no choice. When I do come back we will sit together and set up the proper details of my operation. And until then, my regards to your folks."

Hiltrude was gone in a flash. Welby blinked to make certain she was gone and then he took a finger to each ear to clear them in disbelief of the demands she just made.

Demands he knew deep down he would now fulfill.

◆

Hiltrude now knew everyone in the town of Klackerstack considered her the sweet peasant girl with the hidden past. But that was all about to change. She kept herself busy for the next two days and when the time was right she marched up to Welby's building and barged right in. She didn't even bother to knock. With a push of the door that almost flew off the hinges, she entered. Welby usually let his patients in with a greeting and a smile and was surprised to see such behavior. On this day he was busy finishing up on old man Swayne and his case of the shivers. Welby was applying the last bit of ointment on his back when Hiltrude let herself in. Welby thanked Swayne for coming to him before the shivers spread to all the other areas of his body and excused himself to welcome her. Swayne finished buttoning up his shirt and thanked Welby in return as he left. Swayne walked right past Hiltrude and what normally would have been a simple gesture of a nod hello, for some odd reason he kept his head down refusing to make eye contact with the homely girl that all the others in town whispered about. She looked as if she were on some sort of mission and Swayne wanted no part of it. Hiltrude continued walking toward Welby. By the look on Hiltrude's face, Welby knew at that precise moment his answer to her request for a total facial reconstruction would be yes. In fact any other requests by her would also be yes. Hiltrude walked into his office and sat in one of the two wooden chairs that stood opposite his chair across from his desk.

In no uncertain terms she laid out all the plans for her procedure and the rest of the work she wanted done as well. Welby found himself in some sort of spell he could not explain if anyone would have asked. He just sat down at his chair and took notes. He cleared his schedule for the 21st of the month and penciled in the date. Hiltrude wasted no more precious time of the man who would perform her miracle. She thanked him in that all too familiar stern voice he was now used to. She then stood up, turned around briskly and walked away. In the matter of a minute she was long gone from his sight. Welby sat in his chair for what felt like hours looking totally defeated and feeling totally exhausted.

He couldn't believe he was really going to reconstruct Hiltrude's face. A face that really wasn't as bad as the others in the village whispered about. A face that he hoped he could make beautiful.

◆

That morning Hiltrude woke up exceptionally early. She was too excited about her new appearance that she and Welby had gone over in detail. The surgery was to take place at 10a.m. and would take approximately three to four hours to perform according to Welby.

It would be two weeks before she would be able to move about.

Welby converted the office he had for his other patients into a mini-recovery room with a cot and small dresser. He told her she could stay in the room so he could check and keep tabs on her progress. This delighted Hiltrude. Welby would consult with the other patients in his examination room for the allotted time.

Hiltrude ate a very small breakfast, which consisted of a croissant and freshly squeezed orange juice. She dressed in her very best clothes, which didn't help make her look any more glamorous. She packed a small suitcase and started on her way over to Welby's office. As she walked through town the local townspeople who she thought would have accepted her by now continued to stare without so much as a simple greeting. Hiltrude didn't care. In just a few weeks she would have everyone throughout this town and the surrounding others stopping in their tracks to strike up a conversation with her. Then she would have the last laugh. She would simply ignore them and give them a taste of their own medicine. Hiltrude walked with her head held high. The only thing that she couldn't quite figure out was how a town full of people could accept someone like Welby, who was a stuttering, dumpy, unattractive man, and shun her like she was some sort of pitiful creature.

◆

Welby rose earlier than normal himself. He didn't sleep as well as he would have liked.

The thought of performing a procedure such as the one Hiltrude requested terrified him.

He knew the townspeople respected him and trusted him in his profession but a surgery such as this was all new to him. He would do his darndest to meet her specifications.

For some strange reason he knew he would have to. He couldn't quite put his finger on it as to why the plastic surgery must be his finest work to date. He just had this unnerving feeling that if he didn't, nothing good would come of it. Welby finished eating, dressed and was on his way to his office. Everyone in the village greeted him as he walked down the cobblestone streets. He walked these streets quite often and never tired of the admiration he felt from all the people. Some would run across the street just to say a quick hello while others would give him freshly baked goods from their own houses. Welby, indeed, was a very respected man in his community. Welby, too, now walked with his head held high. Little did he know just how low his head would hang in the weeks to follow.

◆

"Hello, Hiltrude. Are we all set for your big day?" Welby asked as he met up with her in front of his office. Hiltrude handed him her small suitcase and pushed her way past him to lead him into his own office saying, "More than you can ever know, Emdee. You don't mind if I call you Emdee? It came to me in my sleep late last night. After all, you are a doctor. Funny that everyone is this silly village calls you by your first name. Didn't you ever wonder why?"

Welby never even considered being called anything but by his first name. Now this woman standing in front of him questioned all the people in the village that he had known his whole life. In a way, Welby became irritated and responded, "No, actually, Hiltrude I never did give it fought, I mean thought. Yea, thought. Emdee seems so degrading and impersonal. Why not just call me Welby. After ball, all, yea all, why simplify my name and call me by a slang term. Emdee sounds so, so unprofessional. Like a glorified fake of some sort. I dunno know, I can't explain it. I just don't like the term and would much more prefer to be called simply Welby. Now, lets just get you prepped and ready for surgery."

Hiltrude noticed how upset this made him. What was wrong with the name Emdee baffled her. She knew that it hit a nerve with Welby. Or more like a soft spot. Hiltrude liked to confuse him and watch him get all flustered. She followed him into the examination room to prepare herself for the procedure. A life changing procedure. Now as she watched Welby get everything he needed in order to start the long awaited surgery, she lay down on the table as he administered something to put her to sleep. As Hiltrude drifted off into a faraway place where she stood tall and beautiful, she kept repeating the word she knew would bother Welby from this day forward, the name of EMDEE.

◆

Hiltrude woke up feeling groggier than she ever had. Emdee had wheeled her into the newly furnished recovery room, which would now serve as her home for the next couple of weeks. Hiltrude tried to move to see the clock on the wall. The pain she felt by just tilting her head to one side was unbearable. The clock read 3am. She had been out since way before noon. Every inch of her body ached and when she tried to muster up her voice to clear her throat only a squeak came out. She noticed that Emdee had left her a glass of water and what she hoped was some sort of painkiller. It took every ounce of her strength and willpower to reach for the glass and pill. She grimaced in excruciating pain. Twice she almost dropped the glass from the pain that shot through her body just from raising the cup. After what felt like an eternity to raise the cup of water to her lips and place the pill in her mouth, she swallowed the tablet. Hiltrude laid her head back down on the pillow and closed her eyes. The pill took a few minutes to kick in but once it did she felt the pain subsiding. Not as much as she would have liked but enough for her to drift off to sleep. A sleep where SHE was once again the fairest of them all.

◆

Welby looked after her for the next two weeks providing her with all that she required for a speedy recovery. Hiltrude slipped in and out of consciousness and was never fully alert until almost three weeks to the day of the surgery. In that time while she was recuperating, rumors had circulated around the village that Welby was now capable of performing various plastic surgeries. In the three weeks Welby was begged, bartered, financially rewarded, and shamed into doing plastic surgery on at least half of the people in the village. He felt he owed it to them. He worked endless hours to accommodate their needs. He was in his office at the crack of dawn working straight through until the late hours of the evening. In other words, Welby was both physically and mentally drained. He kept up with and was able to complete his demanding schedule. His operations ranged from fixing noses to shortening fingers, to various other external feature adjustments that he never deemed imaginable in all his years of practice. But Welby did the best he could do with what little knowledge in those specific areas that he had. He was finally finished and now he could focus on Hiltrude once again. Her bandages were to be removed first thing the next morning. The others in the town had all seemed pleased with their results and offered him many compliments on their successes. People that really didn't need any enhancements to their faces and bodies now only looked more attractive. Welby laughed when he thought of how this one simple village now looked like a town full of beautiful people, much more desirable to the eye than one could have pictured.

Welby lost himself in thought and was jolted back to reality when he heard a low grunt come from Hiltrude. A moan that sounded more monstrous than human. Welby knew it was only a sound. Deep down Welby knew Hiltrude would be his masterpiece, what he didn't know was that half the other people in town would be more attractive then she.

◆

Welby had not seen Hiltrude for the last four days. Her recovery was long over and he was now back to the basics. No one else in the town came to him with any special requests. Welby was very glad for that and continued in his old style of practice.

Welby was sitting behind his desk again since he turned the recovery room back into his office doing paperwork when Hiltrude stormed in looking very upset. "Look at me Emdee! I mean really look at me! Granted I now stand more erect than I had in the past. My nose is still beaked like that of a bird but not as pointy as it was. And my ears. What in earth were you thinking? Look at these," Hiltrude said looking at herself in the mirror on Welby's wall. "I said make me the fairest of them all. "Have you walked around town Lately? Well have you! Half the people in this damn village are more beautiful than I.

Did you hear what I just said? Half the village you fool!" Hiltrude stood over him staring at him with the most hateful piercing eyes.

Welby started to speak and noticed right away that his voice was shaking when he said, "Now bold on, I mean hold on. You ARE very attractive. Just look at you. I did everything you asked. You're taller, I shortened your nose. I met every specific specification like you basked. Asked, like you asked."

With a very stern voice Hiltrude replied, "Speak properly, you bumbling old fool. Listen to yourself. You can't even pronounce your words. No wonder I look the way I do."

Welby felt his face flush and watched as she continued to stare at him. She then raised her voice and said, "Emdee, you call this beautiful? Granted I look like I can be royalty. I would most definitely fit the part of a Queen. But now, DAMN it, I will have to work at winning over the King of my dreams. I wanted to look like those young girls who walk around this town looking like they stepped out of a pretty line. I can't believe this or you for that matter, Emdee! Someone must pay for this! And trust me, Emdee, it won't be me." Hiltrude said this as she leaned over his desk and leaned her arms on the desk staring into his eyes with a look she knew he had never seen before.

Hiltrude then stood and started towards the door. Welby started to panic and pleaded for her to come back saying, "Come back. Please come back! I did the best I could with what I had to work with."

Hiltrude stopped in her tracks. She turned and glared at him with the meanest look imaginable. She sneered as she spoke, " With what you had to work with! Is that what I just heard you say, Emdee? Oh, believe me, you will pay. And pay dearly, you will. Listen Emdee, and listen closely, I will stop at nothing to destroy you. Put you out of business is mild to what I have planned for you. You screwed up, Emdee, and now you'll pay. A price so dearly. And if I were you, I would watch your back. Because when you least expect it, I will win and my wish will come true. I still am not the most beautiful woman in this town and now I realize it was never your intention to make me so. But your fate is much worse. Trust me, Emdee, much much worse. She then turned around again and headed for the door leading down the steps to the cobblestone street. Welby ran after her with his knees wobbling so badly that he felt he might collapse at any second. When he finally made it to the street, she was gone, as if she simply disappeared. Then out of nowhere he heard a loud shrieking overhead and looked up to see what it was. At least a hundred black crows were circling around his building wildly flapping their wings. They did this for a full minute or two before finally flying off into the distance.

◆

Hiltrude was furious in the weeks that followed. No one in the village had seen her since that day the black crows took over the sky. She would sneak around and stay out of the way of the townspeople. When she was foolish enough to be seen she was always greeted, something she wasn't yet used to, with kind remarks. People said she now looked elegant and stood so tall. Nothing of a beautiful face. She would just dismiss them and move on. Granted she did have the air of elegance. But not nearly enough of the finer qualities in life. Emdee had made her a foot taller and made her body very slender. If only her nose and ears weren't so pointy. Twice she had left the village in the middle of the night and visited a medicine man from a nearby town. He was known to practice witchcraft and even had spells that he was willing to sell. Hiltrude made a very large purchase of various supplies that dealt in sorcery. She in fact, spent most of the money she had ever saved.

She took home all he had put together for her. Hiltrude then concentrated on putting together a spell that would seal Emdee's fate. It took her a full week to perfect her special potion. She mixed many ingredients in a large kettle over a hot fire while chanting in a language that she never knew she could speak. Hiltrude mumbled her words much like how Emdee spoke on a daily basis. All at once she felt transfixed and knew it was precisely the right moment to put in the final touch to her potion. The clock on the wall had just struck midnight. Everyone knew that the witching hour was always at midnight. She took a knife from the table and cut the tip of her finger and let the final process take control. Her blood dripped off her finger and fell into the large kettle. A burst of smoke erupted from the potion and Hiltrude was forced to close her eyes. When she finally did open them she heard the most disturbing screams. Screams coming from outside her window. Scream upon endless scream from many of the townspeople. Hiltrude knew what she must do next. She threw on a black overcoat and headed outside to meet what she hoped would be the results of her magic spell.

People that were once beautiful because of the touch of Emdee's hand were now coming out their doors with a look of horror on their faces. Hiltrude stepped back and looked on in amazement as all the people who had work done on them to look more beautiful now looked like hideous creatures. Men and women had bumps and what looked like burn marks covering their faces. Most of them were hunched over and quite a few limped on what looked like a leg that was shorter than the other. Some of the men were carrying lit torches and others were carrying pitchforks and other weapons of destruction. Hiltrude smiled as she walked into the middle of the street. She took a lantern from one of the deformed women who was crying uncontrollably. Once she felt like everyone who would have been infected by her spell was gathered around her, she waited for them to quiet down. Hiltrude then loudly spoke, "The man you call Welby did this to you. I call him EMDEE. Emdee the quack. Emdee the one who made you the monsters you now are!" A local villager from the back of the congregating crowd screamed, "How could this happen to us? I say we go find him and ask him ourselves! Better still I say we make him pay for this! Look what he did to us."

One woman starting screaming all over again, which moved the others to anger as well.

A riot from the now angered mob was about to start. Hiltrude knew she had their full attention and knew that the next statement she made would fulfill the promise of revenge she had made to Emdee. She carefully planned what she would say and yelled at the top of her lungs, "Hang the bastard, pull him out of his house and tie him to the nearest tree."

Hiltrude let it all sink in for the next minute or so. Just as she was about to make another suggestion of what to use for this task, she noticed a man who looked worse than any of the others in the mob run up to her with a rope in the shape of a noose.

Hiltrude lead the group of hysterical people screaming as she ran, "Kill the Emdee! Kill the Emdee!"

The others all joined in her chant. Emdee, no longer Welby. They were all screaming out Emdee. A name that Welby truly disliked. A name that would remain with him forever.

◆

Welby was up much later than he had expected. Usually he was fast asleep by ten o'clock in the evening and it was now minutes before midnight and he was just finishing his paperwork that he needed for the office. He stood up and walked into the bathroom and looked into the mirror. He, too, knew he wasn't an attractive man with his pudgy round face and shorter than normal body. His glasses and long white beard were anything but appealing. As he stood there staring at his reflection in the mirror a sudden uneasiness came over him. He couldn't remember the last time he had seen Hiltrude or heard from her. Just the thought of that horrible confrontation weeks ago sent shivers up his spine.

But since then, he hadn't heard a peep from her. He thought for sure she would have retaliated by now and he once again shivered. She promised to destroy his practice. How she could manage that baffled Welby. Welby thought that maybe over time she had come to terms with herself. After all she did look a thousand times better than she did when he first met her. But then again he felt that odd feeling. A feeling he couldn't explain. Welby turned away from his mirror just as the clock struck midnight.

He fussed around his bedroom for the next couple of minutes before deciding to change into his bedclothes for hopefully a good night's sleep. He hadn't had a restful sleep since that day when Hiltrude threatened to seek revenge. Again a feeling of uneasiness came over him when a pound instead of a knock came at his front door.

Welby ran to answer as he now heard distant screams coming from somewhere outside.

As he opened the door he was surprised to see both his momma and papa standing there with a look of terror in their eyes. Marcel watched the scene take place in the middle of the street where Hiltrude masterminded her plan. He grabbed hold of his wife and they snuck into the night to warn Welby. Welby ushered them in. The screams were fast approaching. Marcel and Marisol wasted no time in telling what had happened. They urged him to flee as fast as possible knowing what the outcome for their only child would be. Marcel swore to hold off the angry crowd. Welby was paralyzed with fear.

Never in his wildest imagination would he have thought this to be the revenge Hiltrude could cause. Marisol threw together a couple of items in a knapsack and handed it to him.

All three then headed out of the house and down his steps to the cobblestone street.

Off in the distance, no more than a block away at most, Welby saw what would haunt him forever. Hiltrude was leading a large mob of what looked like monsters. Very grotesque ones. Most were carrying something. Torches, pitchforks and what looked like a rope in the shape of a noose. All of a sudden it hit Welby. Hiltrude had done something to these people. These people whom he was sure he performed the surgery on to enhance their beauty. Hiltrude had cast some evil spell and had succeeded and now he was to pay the ultimate price. The cost of his life. Hiltrude had won. Welby was going to be killed by this angry mob. Most of whom were not only his patients but also his friends. Hiltrude had turned them into these creatures and now she turned them against him. Marcel and Marisol, his parents, wasted no time. They said a quick and loving goodbye to their only son whom they knew, they would never see again.

Welby hugged them both and took a tighter hold of the knapsack. He knew his parents wouldn't be harmed. After all they had no part in it and there were still many other normal townspeople who, if his parents were in danger, would come to their rescue. In fact many of the normal townspeople were starting to come outdoors to see what all the commotion was. Marcel and Marisol went to meet the normal ones to put a stop to the angry crowd. Welby, on the other hand, knew he would have to leave never to return because the whole village would become one giant battlefield until he was finally lynched for something he didn't do. To Welby life seemed so unfair. He took off in the other direction. He ran as fast as his little legs would carry him. He knew where he must head and he ran straight toward it never looking back as he ran. Welby gave up a good life and loving parents.

He ran and ran until he reached the outskirts of the Black Forest.

4

Cranky walked over to Emdee who was standing in front of his bed just staring into space and gently tapped him on the shoulder asking, "Emdee, wake up. Are you in there?" Emdee snapped out of his trance. Cranky continued, "Whew, I thought we lost you there for a minute. Were ya deep in thought? Where'd ya go Emdee?"

Emdee didn't answer. He did notice, however, that there was no one hiding in his bed. He stepped aside to let Cranky examine his bed. Cranky couldn't believe how ashen and ghostlike Emdee appeared. Cranky figured that whatever Emdee was thinking sure took its toll on him. Cranky was next in line to check his bed while the others now formed a circle around their beloved Emdee concerned for his well-being. As Emdee tried in vain to ease the others concern for him, Cranky tip-toed up to his bed. He reached down with both hands and pulled the sheets back off his bed when he was struck with a vivid flashback. Many flashbacks all at once that he, too, tried to block from his memory. Cranky was frozen in place. All he could do was just stand there as images from his past came flashing through his mind. A mind that was so tormented many years ago.

Sheldon Ebony

For this little man who will never be tall or lanky,
So he shall be given the name of CRANKY.........

-Esperanza

5

Once upon a time far, far away there was an infant boy born of small measures. His parents were shocked to see their child born so tiny. Raphael and Anastasia Ebony, his parents, lived in a farmhouse about a mile away from the border of the village, Linderstaff. To survive, and earn income, Raphael raised turkeys and slaughtered them to sell to the people of the town. Anastasia helped with the chores around the farm tending to the other animals they owned. The pigs, horses and even the two milking cows kept both of them very busy. The Ebony's had two other sons before their third son was born. Their first two sons were much larger and of average size when they were each delivered and the fact that their third son was so tiny concerned both his parents right away. They had given their third son the name of Sheldon after Anastasia's father. As Sheldon grew in age from infant to young toddler he really didn't grow much in height.

Raphael was alarmed by his under development and became more and more distant from Sheldon as the young toddler became a little boy. Raphael, also chose to spend more time showing his other two sons how to work around the farm. He shied away from Sheldon, and barely spoke to him at all. Sheldon's mother was worse. Anastasia was most upset over his inability to grow and found herself showering her two older boys with love and affection. Whenever Sheldon went up to hug his mother, she would always pretend that she was busy doing some kind of chore around their home. Sheldon knew even at an early age that his mother chose to shun him rather than love him. The only woman in a house of men made this discomforting to poor young Sheldon. From an early age, Sheldon started to despise his mother in return. He didn't know much about the opposite sex but what he knew about his mother was enough to make him dislike any woman. Sheldon grew or as his parents would state, aged, and with his under development his attitude changed too. His personality was that of a loner due to the fact that he was basically ignored in his household. What little hope of understanding and caring about him was left up to his two older brothers, Lupus and Theo. Both his brothers stood over six feet tall and were blond and blue-eyed. His parents treated them like Gods. Around the farm, Lupus and Theo, were given the easy chores, while Sheldon, from an early age, had to work in the slaughterhouse. At first, Sheldon liked turkeys almost to the point that he wanted one as a pet. When his brothers heard of this, they teased him relentlessly. Sheldon was used to his brothers picking on him. As all three of them became young men, Sheldon grew a beard first. His two brothers didn't even need to shave. His beard came in fully white like that of an old man and this too embarrassed his parents more. Sheldon knew he was different and only wished his family were more compassionate to him, which of course they weren't. Lupus and Theo had chosen to ridicule and tease him whenever the opportunity arose, which was more often than not. From as early as Sheldon could remember, his brothers found it quite funny at his expense to call him silly names and make fun of his height. Sheldon learned to grin and bear it. What hurt more than anything was that sometimes when his brothers picked on him and when he looked for his mother to defend him, he found her laughing along with them. This further confirmed his hatred of women. Sheldon knew women couldn't be trusted, especially when his own mother could be so cold. His father would on very rare occasions put a stop to the constant teasing only when he realized that Sheldon was truly upset. Most of the time Sheldon wouldn't show his emotions and hid them under a grim disposition. As he got older he learned to hide all his emotions. He didn't want to give his brothers or his mother the satisfaction that they were hurting his feelings when in actuality it did. Sheldon would run off behind their house to the barn and throw himself into the haystack and cry out loud. He knew he was out of earshot and sometimes his sobbing would sound very loud. As he became a young man his life at home was unbearable. His mother continued to dote upon Lupus and Theo and basically ignored him. His papa never paid him no mind. Sheldon hated everything about his family. He longed for the village of Linderstaff and for the comfort of other people. As his disposition worsened, a coping method he used in order to exist in his household, he knew that he wouldn't be much more sociable around others in the village either. He knew he was destined to spend his life around these miserable people known as his family. His papa made him work long hours in the turkey slaughterhouse doing the jobs that he detested. Sheldon had to slit the turkey's throats while his papa held them down. Sheldon loved these animals at first but as the years progressed and he butchered them right alongside his papa, he pitied them in the end. The only thing about the turkeys that comforted him before he sliced open their necks was that theirs was an easy death unlike the misery and suffering he went through with each passing day. His papa made him also clean the blood off the floors everyday before calling it a night. Many an evening Sheldon would have to scrub his hands until he felt like the skin would peel off just to get the embedded bloodstains cleaned. As he became older he became more and more bitter. He truly was an unhappy person. His face had now taken on a frown that even he couldn't make vanish. All those long years of punishment he had suffered at the hands of his beloved family made the frown permanent. On more than one occasion he would interrupt family conversations just to argue or start a disagreement with one of them. This had become his only pleasure. If a fistfight with either

Lupus or Theo erupted, then he knew he had won. At least in the sense of the word. For such a short man he put up a real fight. Only when it was one on one was he able to duke it out, but usually both his older brothers would come to each other's defense and poor Sheldon suffered the consequences. Sheldon had many bruises and black eyes over the years that he would have to tend to himself. His mother was never around when he needed bandaging but always appeared when her two older sons were hurt. Sheldon longed for a day when he would leave knowing full well that his parents would never allow it.

The Ebony family lived in a modest farmhouse. The kitchen, living room and the one bedroom were on the first floor while there were two bedrooms on the second floor. Raphael had built the house himself using wood from the trees off his land. As a young and newly married man, Raphael, was quite the builder. Both his parents and brothers slept in the upstairs bedrooms leaving him downstairs in the other bedroom by himself at night alone. During many a storm when Sheldon was little he would run upstairs only to be told that there was no room in his parent's bed for him since Lupus and Theo were already nestled between them. Sheldon battled many a thunderstorm by himself when he was certain witches and goblins were lurking within them. He became independent at an early age too. That was why Sheldon kept to himself and never smiled. As he got older, he found he could no longer smile. So much bitterness and anger was built up in him. He longed to visit the village just as Lupus and Theo did to sell the turkeys to the other townspeople. That was never an option for him. He knew his parents would be the laughing stock of the village if they saw their third son of such small proportions. Only Lupus and Theo who were envied by all the other young men in their village because of their good looks could venture into town. Anastasia would join them on occasion just to watch the local girls swoon in her sons' presence. Sheldon figured that was why his mother home schooled him while his brothers were able to attend the village school. They all wanted to keep him a secret from the villagers. The village that consisted of no more than three hundred families and a total of fourteen hundred people. His mother told him that only two children from each family could be sent to the town school, leaving him the wrath of his mother. If Sheldon was taught for more than six hours a week it was six hours too many for his mother. Her patience was short and she barely looked at him when she spoke. Anastasia put up with him and the very limited teaching only to keep Sheldon far away from what she knew would be total humiliation for the rest of the Ebony family. Sheldon not only didn't grow in height, he also was stunted in his ability to learn making him all the more uneducated as well. Raphael knew everyone in town since he provided them with the only turkeys available. On the few occasions that the Ebony family did visit town for Church services, Sheldon was given the afternoon off. Raphael kept him so exhausted that Sheldon was too tired to go to Sunday service. He used that as an excuse knowing his parents would never allow him to go along. From an early age, they kept him far away from the village of Linderstaff and very hidden when on a few occasions villagers would stop by to pay a visit. His mother knew in advance when they were going to stop by and made sure her husband put Sheldon to work in the slaughterhouse behind the barn far away from anyone's view. Sheldon would sometimes peek out the tiny window just to see what other people looked like. He knew they couldn't see him even if they wanted too since it was so far from the house. His father, however, wanted to take no chances and when Sheldon was caught doing this the whipping was much more painful than a quick glimpse out the small window was worth. To Sheldon it wasn't worth the risk of the beating that would follow and he had since given up on even trying. Sheldon, in fact, couldn't remember the last time he saw another human being other than his parents and two brothers. But that was all about to change, since Sheldon was about to meet the person who would change his life forever.

◆

Sheldon watched as his parents and two brothers left for their mile walk to Church service on that hazy, hot, and humid Sunday morning. Sheldon had come to dislike his family more and more each passing day and as he watched them walk together into the distance, he was glad to have the peace and quiet of being alone. After all, even when they were around him it felt like he was invisible. Sheldon returned to bed to sleep knowing fully that the next six days would be anything but restful.

His papa lined up more chores than he was capable of doing in the turkey slaughterhouse.

Sheldon basically ran the whole operation within those blood soaked walls. His papa spent more and more time outside with his golden sons, Lupus and Theo. Sheldon preferred when his papa remained outside and made sure to do everything he could to resist his demands when they did work together inside the slaughterhouse.

Sheldon now lay there thinking just how miserable his life really was. He knew it was all due to his small stature and only wished his family could have been supportive instead of abusive. As Sheldon was just about to doze off, he heard a pounding at the front door. Startled at first, then composed, he sat up in bed. Sheldon knew company never came unannounced enabling his mother to make sure that he was sent off to work never to be seen. Sheldon tried to keep his anxiety under control but with the constant knocking at their front door it was beginning to unnerve him. Whoever was knocking wouldn't stop and the persistence had Sheldon on edge. He quietly tiptoed over to the door. Sheldon didn't know if he should even dare to take a peek through the side window to see who the impatient visitor was. Sheldon reached over and lightly moved the white lace curtain to the side. Because of his size, he was unable to see out the window and he had to step up on his toes to look over the windowsill. What Sheldon saw at first shocked him. Delivering this loud knock was a tiny woman. As soon as Sheldon first looked at her their eyes locked onto eachother. Sheldon determined that she had to be an old woman because she was much older looking than his mother.

He was about to let go of the curtain for he knew that she too had now spotted him. Sheldon didn't even want to know what his wrath would be when this old woman went back to the village and started telling everyone about the short man who lived in the Ebony household. Sheldon started to perspire and shake. As he was about to turn away he heard the old woman call out to him through the window, "Well, just how long will you make an old woman stand out here in the heat before you open the door?"

Sheldon didn't answer when she spoke again, "Open up. I know you're in there and I ain't leavin' till you let me in. I know your mother and papa and those sorry excuses for brothers left for Sunday service. Now at least come to the door."

Sheldon was confused. If he walked away she was bound to leave eventually and return to town and Sheldon pushed away the rest of the outcome from his mind. But on the other hand, if he let her in, what would he say to the old woman? From the quick glimpse of her, she couldn't be all that much taller than he was. She had long scraggly white hair, and a face that could scare the wits out of you on a dark lonely night. She was also very hunched over which was another sign of her old age. For one split second his heart went out to her. She really did look scary. As he made his way back to the door to open, he worried that whatever happened next, things couldn't get any worse.

◆

Sheldon put his hand on the doorknob right after he wiped the sweat off his palm on his shirt before turning it. He hated women because of his mother and knew nothing good would come of this. He stepped back after he opened the door to let the full view of the old woman come into sight. He didn't have a chance to utter a word before she spoke again, "Thought you was gonna keep me out their all day. I wasn't gonna leave til ya let me in anyhows. Now where can an old lady like myself take a load off her feet?"

Sheldon was shocked at the blunt manner in which this old woman spoke, and once again it confirmed his distrust of the opposite sex. Sheldon who was so used to now speaking his mind in front of his family found it hard to make a sentence as he said, "If you saw my family leave, then how did you know anyone else was home. Especially me?"

The old woman looked him up and down as she made her way to the dining room table where she sat herself down and replied, "I know all about you and don't start asking me all these questions. Just trust me. The name's Esperanza." She scratched her chin before continuing to speak and said, "Sheldon. Yes, that's it. Sheldon. Well Sheldon. Why aren't you at Church service with your family?" knowing well what the answer was.

Sheldon gaped at her in disbelief. First she used the word trust when indeed he knew he could never trust any woman. And secondly, she knew his name. Baffled, Sheldon asked, "But how do you know my name? And what is it you want? We don't sell no turkeys on Sunday." Sheldon started to feel his oats again, "Besides that's what my brothers do. They bring the turkey into town to drop off at all the different houses."

Esperanza watched him gain his confidence back, "What, no hello, nice to meet ya? Where'd ya get your manners boy? I ain't here for no turkeys. Besides those two turkeys you call brothers, Lupus and Theo, don't know their behinds from their elbows."

Sheldon felt his grin twitch. He always frowned but for just an instant he almost smiled.

Something he couldn't ever remember doing. Calling Lupus and Theo turkeys. Yes, that truly was a good description of them. One he was sure he would never forget.

◆

Sheldon and Esperanza sat together at the table for at least a half hour making small talk before the old woman stated the real reason behind her visit, "Sheldon, are ya game for a little fun? Ya just told me ya ain't never been off this pitiful farm. What'ya say we walk on over and take a peek at your village?"

Sheldon looked at her for what felt like hours when he answered, "Are you crazy old woman? Ain't YOU been listening to everything I just told you. My papa

48

would give me a lashing I would never forget. Sneak into town and do what?"

"We don't have to go into town. We could go to the woods over by old man Gusby's farm, which has a full view of the streets in town. We'll take a seat on an old log and just people watch. You can see what other people look like and what they do," Esperanza said giving it everything she had to convince Sheldon.

"What, I mean, my poppa and mother might see me. I'm afraid, Esperanza," Sheldon pleaded with fear in his eyes.

Esperanza took pity on this poor soul and continued, "Don't ya want to see what you been missing. What your miserable family kept ya from all these years! What'ya say kid.

How 'bout it? You and I go sneak a peek? Remember, you CAN trust me Sheldon."

Trust her. This old woman who only until two hours ago never existed. Sheldon was troubled. On one hand he didn't trust her but on the other hand a visit to a town he only dreamt of was a great temptation. Sheldon had nothing to lose and only time on his hands. His family never came right back anyhow. It would be hours before they returned home. Perhaps a quick look would do him good. After all, Sheldon had never seen the town that his two brothers so frequently visited. How bad could it be Sheldon thought, if Lupus and Theo the turkeys, enjoyed it so much. Sheldon then decided it was worth the risk to take a peek from the outside looking in to see just what all the fuss about this village was. The worst-case scenario, Sheldon would wind up in the turkey slaughterhouse on the receiving line this time.

◆

"Yeah, lets do it! I say we leave right now," Sheldon said pushing back his chair at the table and jumping up. "What do I have to lose? Can't get any worse for me," he continued excitedly.

Esperanza tried to keep a serious expression instead of the smile she was hiding within as she answered him, "Now ya talking! She slapped her hand on her lap and continued, "Help me up out of this chair and let's get goin'. We have some distance to cover and a lot to see."

◆

Sheldon followed Esperanza as they made their way through the woods and to the village that he now so desired to see. Sheldon felt his heart palpitating and the adrenaline rush was fascinating to him. He longed for his first glimpse at the village of Linderstaff. For such an old woman she walked at a fast speed. At times it was more like a slow run, which more than once caused Sheldon to find himself trying to keep up. Esperanza came to a complete stop. Her plan was about to unfold. If everything went according to her timing, Esperanza would succeed giving back to the Ebony family what they deserved. Like that long ago night when she was starving and came to the Ebony house begging for a smitten of food only to be turned away by Sheldon's papa. Raphael took one look at her and forced her from his land. More like threatened her if she didn't leave right away. Esperanza still felt the pain. The next farm, which wasn't all that much further down the road took her in, fed her, and gave her a place to sleep regardless of her outside appearance. Now the Ebony family had secrets of their own. Secrets are never good and can ultimately destroy one's soul. Much like the tortured soul, she endured. Now they too would share the pain they had inflicted on their third son. Esperanza had followed the Ebony family for years in order to one day seek revenge for that haunted night from her past. Many a day, over the years, from a distance behind their house she watched and watched as their third son of such small measure was treated just like her. Sheldon would be the one to finalize her plan. Sheldon would play his most important role yet. She vowed to one day pay them back. And today what Sheldon would see would most certainly help move it all along. Not only for her, but also for Sheldon who now stood next her too. As she pushed those thoughts back into memory, she turned to face him and said in a whisper, "See beyond those there trees? Old man Gusby's farm is right there yonder. Should be there in no more than five minutes. Now keep up and remember to stay out of sight."

Sheldon had no problem staying out of sight. After all, he had been doing that his whole life.

◆

Sheldon was more brazen now that he could possibly have imagined. Just moments ago Esperanza said they would be on the property of an old man whose name Sheldon was too excited to remember. She came up alongside of him and pointed around what looked like a barn. "We just have to go right up next to that there barn and you'll get a full view of the village. Now hurry up and follow me," Esperanza said speaking more quickly than Sheldon was used to. The two of them gaped out from the side of the barn where they could clearly see the streets and all the activities of what a busy village life was like. People of all shapes and sizes and various hair colors were all walking, laughing and even just standing around looking to have a swell time. Everyone seemed to Sheldon to be so relaxed. No one or anyone for that matter was tense. The day may have been hazy and hot but it didn't keep the villagers indoors. Sheldon was awestruck.

He sat down on a log that lay next to the barn and stared in astonishment at all that he'd been missing. All that he ever really longed for. And as Esperanza had hoped, she had even timed it precisely knowing what would be happening in the town of Linderstaff, the annual end of the summer festival. It was the biggest and most festive event yet in all the years of the town of Linderstaff's existence. Esperanza sat there as Sheldon moved closer to her to see all the fuss. Villagers were dressed in costumes garnished in bright colors Sheldon had never seen before. Some stood taller than he ever imagined possible with some sort of flag or banner waving from side to side in the air. Children much like he once was were following these tall people, on what now appeared to be wood poles attached to their legs, all around the streets. Women of various shapes, mostly plump and round, were throwing flowers from baskets into the streets as they too danced to music that Sheldon had never listened to before. The music was festive and loud and had all the townspeople up and about. It seemed like an enormous celebration of some sort of which he would love to have been part of. Oh, how Sheldon truly despised his parents for sheltering, no, more like keeping him from all these festivities. Life in the village was perfect, much more perfect than his life at home. No sooner did he finish that thought when out of the corner of his eye he saw his family. Younger, prettier girls surrounded both Lupus and Theo as the girls danced around them in a seductive way that brought up an urge in Sheldon that he had never experienced. An urge that would make him continue to hate the opposite sex. Both his brothers were smiling from cheek to cheek. His mother and papa followed gloating in the attention bestowed on their two good-looking sons. The whole scene Sheldon witnessed had now turned his stomach. A feeling of bile started to make its way up his throat. Sheldon was going to be sick. He quickly turned from the happiest experience his eyes had ever seen to look for a spot where he could throw up. And as he stood up to make his way over to a tree to heave what little food he had in his belly, he never noticed the smile now spread across Esperanza's face.

◆

Twenty minutes later Esperanza was still comforting Sheldon who was bent over dry heaving. Esperanza knew she had devised her best plan of action and watching Sheldon puke up his poor brains confirmed that she had indeed won.

She now placed both her hands on each of his shoulders to reconfirm what she already knew by softly stating, "There, there, Sheldon. Everything thing will be okay. Too much for ya to absorb in one day. Perhaps we should head back."

Sheldon straightened his back from the position of being hunched over and answered her in his usual sarcastic tone, "Did you see all those people. Laughing, dancing and having so much fun. Is it always like that in town?"

"But of course. Everyday is one big celebration. People love the village and all they do is have parties like that each and every day. Don't let that bother ya Sheldon. I know you feel like ya have been cheated from all these festivities your whole life. And the truth of the matter is is that ya have been. Poor, poor, Sheldon. My heart goes out to you. Must really, really hurt doesn't it?" Esperanza repeated over and over for the next few moments letting her words sink in for full effect.

Sheldon glared at her with eyes of pure hatred when the next words he spoke solidified the deal for her revenge, "Curse them all! All these years they've kept me at home working like THEIR slave instead of their own flesh and blood. Their SON! I curse the day I was born. No, I curse the day they were born. Oh, Esperanza, they will pay for all this misery I have suffered at their hands over the years. Each and every one of them will pay!"

Esperanza whispered softly in his ear as she helped him to his feet for their journey back to Sheldon's farm, "Yes, dear, They each will pay. I will make sure of that. Trust me they will."

◆

Sheldon was back at the farm in plenty of time. Esperanza left right away wasting no time except to promise that she would return over the next few weeks. Sheldon waved her a glad goodbye, silently cursing her under his breath for exposing him to a world of unknowns. He then waited at the dining room table with bated breath for his hateful family to return. He wanted to confront them to ask them one simple question.

If he got the answer he knew that he would, he didn't want to even think of what the outcome would be. An outcome of pure evil that not even he wanted to think about.

◆

"Why, the sudden curiosity of what OUR visit to the village was like? You've never asked before, why now?" His mother inquired still not answering him.

With a tone of voice that Anastasia had never heard before and which somewhat scared her, Sheldon repeated his question again, "What is the village like, Mother? What do YOU do there exactly after Church services?"

His papa was starting to get irritated with his youngest son's tone of voice, but Anastasia, shushed him and finally answered, "Nothing you would care to know about.

After Church services we visit OUR friends for a quiet day of relaxation away from this house and away from YOU." Anastasia knew the last few words would hurt him most and that was why she chose her words carefully as she, too, spoke them in a harsh reply back to Sheldon. Sheldon looked at all four of his family just smirking after the statement his mother had just made. He even caught Lupus smiling from the last point she made about being away from him. Him. The only person in this hateful union of a family that was never given a fair chance. Sheldon received the answer, which was the lie he knew she would tell him, avoiding the festivities they took part in, he turned his head and walked away. The four of them stood there waiting for some rude comment to escape his lips. When Sheldon said nothing, Anastasia knew she had defeated this sorry excuse for a son. What she didn't realize was how close she was becoming to a fate that was much more spiteful.

◆

Sheldon never tired of the visits from Esperanza. In time, he even forgave her for the one and only time he ventured into the village to bear witness to all the glory he missed out on. Esperanza seemed to materialize out of nowhere just minutes after his family would leave for the village on an early Sunday morning. For hours they would walk around the farm talking and sharing in the care for the animals. Esperanza liked to help feed the animals while Sheldon chopped up apples and corn into little pieces to be placed in their bowls. Animals and Sheldon didn't shy away from her like most other people did, making her stay with Sheldon all the more pleasurable. Today, however, was the day Esperanza needed to plant her own seed. A seed that she was sure wouldn't need much watering. A seed that was certain to become the root of all evil.

◆

"Have you thought much about the old village? What'ya had been missing?

You haven't ever mentioned it to me since that day so many months ago," Esperanza asked hoping for the answer she knew would follow.

"I hate them! Why'd ya have to spoil such a pleasant afternoon? They treat me worse than ever. Ever since I asked about what they do there, my family doesn't even acknowledge me anymore. Not that they ever did, but now, not a word if they don't have to," Sheldon said as he finished cutting up the tiny red apple.

"If only I could teach them a lesson or better still put them out of my life for good," Sheldon voiced in his most angry tone.

Esperanza chose her words very carefully knowing just how delicate the conversation was going, "Just by your facial expressions, I can see how angry you are. You look so," she hesitated when the word she had been thinking for oh so long came to mind.

"Cranky, by gone it! That's what ya are kid, Cranky. Ain't never seen anything even come close to a smile on that their face of yours. Because you're so, that's what I'll call ya, CRANKY!"

Pleased by her last statement, she let the new name sink into Sheldon.

Cranky. Sheldon guessed all along that the name Cranky was more of a match than anything else imaginable. After all, life was anything else but Cranky for him.

Esperanza continued, "So just how do ya plan on getting them out of your life for good?

Do you need me to help ya? Ya know I'd be right there by your side in whatever you decide to do every inch of the way."

Cranky looked into her eyes with his most serious stare yet, "Leave, I'll just leave them for good. I'll go live in town and never come back!"

Esperanza laughed at his foolish statement, "Leave and never come back! Your papa along with those two turkeys for brothers would come after ya and drag ya back for good. Maybe even tie ya up and never let you go free no more."

Sheldon hadn't considered that as an outcome and asked, "Do you think they would do that to me? Tie me up for good?"

"You bet ya! To get away for good, you need to rid yourself of the problem," she said.

"And just how do you suppose I do that?" Sheldon inquired.

"KILL them! The whole rotten bunch. Be free of them for good. Once and for all," Esperanza pushed.

"Kill them. How...? By myself...? When...? What would I use...?" Sheldon asked pleading for her to answer right away.

"I'll help ya, Cranky. Carve 'em up as they sleep in their beds. Make it like they are turkeys. Slice THEIR necks. You take your mother and I'll take your papa. Then we'll go after those two turkeys next. Your brothers. They should be easy. They're turkeys already. Don't think about it. I'll show up the night after tomorrow, say around the stroke of midnight, and knock on ya window. You let me in and the rest will be easy.

I promise ya. You and me Cranky. You can trust me on that."

Sheldon couldn't believe what he was hearing. Trust was such a strong word. A word he was never comfortable with. Esperanza had his trust. Could he have hers was his uncertainty. Sheldon wanted nothing more than to be rid of his family.

He would no longer have to work, answer, or look at them when they looked at him like he was some sort of freak. Sheldon could finally be free of them and all the hardship he endured at their hands over the years. All he needed to do was kill them. As simple as that with the help of Esperanza. Be rid of them all. Sheldon turned to face Esperanza and with what he knew was the closest thing to a smile on his face said, "I think we know what course to follow!"

◆

The next two days dragged on forever. As always, Sheldon was treated in his usual fashion making the task at hand seem all the easier. His mother and papa did everything for Lupus and Theo leaving him like the animal they felt he was.

After dinner, Sheldon cleaned up the table and washed the dishes. He placed them in the cupboards. He finished drying the utensils and as he carefully placed them in the drawer he removed the two largest butcher knives. He made a point to bring them from the turkey slaughterhouse yesterday convincing his papa that they needed a good scrubbing and sharpening. Sheldon took the two knives and headed for his bedroom with the intention of putting them to good use in only a couple of hours. Lying in bed he heard the usual humdrum from the two bedrooms upstairs. His mother and papa along with his two brothers shared in their usual evening of laughter and stories. Sheldon tried to concentrate on something else. He waited until it was silent and then looked over at the clock in his room. In less than two hours at the stroke of midnight he would be free. Free to finally explore the town with all the glory. The town of Linderstaff.

◆

It was never his intention, but Sheldon had dozed off to sleep. In his dream, Sheldon had a premonition of the repercussions of the bloodbath he would be performing.

He was running and running never free to stop. Murdering his family weighed heavily on everyone he came in contact with and his life would be spent as a fugitive on the run. Always running, with never a place to settle down. Every and any where he stopped people would know of the brutal acts he committed and would want to put a stop to him from committing any future murders. His life would never be the same again. Linderstaff would never accept him nor would any other town for that matter. Murder was a crime punishable by death. A death Sheldon was not ready for. A death no one was ever ready for. Certainly not his hated family either.

◆

A slight tapping at his bedroom window startled his restless sleep. Sheldon opened his eyes exactly as the clock struck midnight. He knew who waited just outside his window and he knew just what would come if he opened the window to let her in. The plan that he had gone over so many times in his head these past two days, a plan that he knew he would now never be able to carry out. Oh so quietly he stepped down off his bed. He knew Esperanza couldn't see in since his curtains were drawn. Sheldon opened up his bedroom drawers and took out a couple of pieces of clothing and packed them in his blanket. He wrapped the blanket up into a pouch and tossed it over his shoulder. He left the knives hidden under his mattress with no intention of now using them. He lightly walked out his bedroom door listening to another light tapping on his glass. Esperanza who masterminded the whole demise of his family kept on knocking, like that day long ago when she first took him into the village. Back when he did trust her. Sheldon knew at that precise moment that he would never open the window to let the evil that he once trusted in. A trust that was not easy for him. Sheldon now picked up his pace and headed for the front door. He never glanced back at his window or even upstairs to where his hateful family slept. He knew they would be unharmed by the evil knocking at his window. Even for everything they put him through they didn't deserve the cruelty he once wished on them. Esperanza talked him into it and needed him to complete her destiny. A destiny from which he now ran. He opened the door and ran off into the woods to a place he didn't know existed. A place where he could be free. Free to be himself.

Sheldon ran into the night and straight toward the Black Forest.

6

Emdee noticed Cranky not moving, much like himself only moments ago. He quickly went up to him sensing some sort of spell coming over them one by one. While he was busy awakening Cranky with a push on his arm, Dozzey walked past the two of them and stood in front of his bed now mesmerized just as he and Cranky were minutes before. Emdee knew it was some sort of spell, of that he was certain. Emdee pulled on Cranky's arms who at last started to stir. Emdee whispered into Cranky's ear, "Hang in there, Cranky, you'll feel wetter, ah, better in just a second. Something strange is happening to us. Look over at Dozzey. He hasn't moved since he stood next to his bed. What should we do?"

A puzzled expression came across Cranky's face as he stepped back pulling on Emdee to move back to the door of their bedroom. Dozzey didn't sense any commotion taking place around him. The only commotion was inside his head from a long ago memory. Dozzey raised his arms up in the air to stretch as fear on his face now replaced the yawn the other six were used to.

Rutherford Baccus

This little man will always rest so cozy,
So he shall be given the name of DOZZEY.

-Inga

7

In a distant land many miles away; an infant of small dimensions came to be. The baby boy was loved instantly by his parents and given the name of Rutherford after the village that he was born in. Barker and Sela Baccus, Rutherford's parents, loved the town they chose to settle in. With a population of over four thousand villagers it was one of the most populated of all the surrounding villages. The town had every store or shop one could desire. Two banks, many saloons, a barbershop, candy store, even a general store graced the many streets leading to the Town's Square. A candle factory bordered the corner of Main street, which was the first building of the many attached to one another. The town was crowded at all hours of the day. Villagers lazily walked from one store to another on any given afternoon to browse and for most to purchase items needed to exist in a town as larger as theirs. For Barker and Sela, baby Rutherford was their pride and joy.

As he was their only child, he was spoiled from the moment he was conceived. Many a night, Barker and Sela would talk to her belly, as it grew with each passing month, about all the day's events. Sela loved the child she nurtured in her body and everyone in the village knew this. She was the first to stop a neighbor on her block to strike up a conversation, which usually ended up in discussion of her pregnancy. Sela was a beautiful woman with long brown hair and light green eyes who stood tall at five feet ten inches. Barker, who was six years her senior, had black hair and blue eyes. He, too, was tall. He towered over his tall wife by at least four inches. So it surprised them when Rutherford was born so tiny. He wasn't more than ten inches tall, which their midwife said wasn't unheard of. Seeing their perplexed faces when she held little Rutherford up in the air after he was delivered, she reassured both of them that he would grow just like any other little boy. Knowing that the midwife was reputable throughout the village they took her words as golden. What concerned them more than his itsy-bitsy build was how often he napped. Rutherford slept through most of the night and two-thirds of the day. Sela had to wake him up for feedings and no sooner did he finish a bottle he was once again fast asleep. Barker joked that between the two of them and the hectic schedules they both had prior to Rutherford's birth, their constant running around must have made him tire as he grew within his mother's womb. Still, as Rutherford aged from month to month, the frame of his body stayed the same. So did his sleep habits. Sela was alarmed by his constant falling asleep whenever he could and she asked the midwife as well as the town's doctors if it was something she needed to be concerned about. After a complete examination by each of them they all told her the same diagnosis. Rutherford was a very healthy boy. No physical or mental disabilities other than his stunted growth, which really didn't bother either Barker or Sela. Rutherford was their world and everyone knew that. The doctors stated that each baby was different and since he was born so small, he may require more sleep than other babies who were larger. Sela took their answers as fact and never questioned Rutherford's need for sleep again. As time went on, his parents learned to accept that he would be short of stature and still paraded him around the village they so loved so deeply that they named him after it. Rutherford's constant need to rest his eyes in a peaceful sleep came to be a normal function as well for the infant. Barker and Sela adjusted their lives around his need for down time. People admired both Barker and Sela for the attractive couple they were and for the inspiration they provided to the village. Knowing their love for this booming town, many friends and neighbors had nominated Barker for Mayor. At first he refused but after much coaxing decided that he knew what he wanted for this town and all the people who lived within it. Now, on his second term he proved to be a suitable choice. They lived in a modest wood home just two blocks from the center of town. The whole town was built from the wood of the surrounding hillside. Main Street was one wood building after the other all attached in a row. Everyone in the village capable of working held jobs and not only was the town prospering, but the nearest two towns proved profitable from their village as well. Townsfolk from other towns offering only a meager existence came to Rutherford to seek a better way of life.

Sela, up until having her only son, worked in charitable committees. She provided aid to the elderly when it came to medical assistance. She scheduled means of transportation for the sick and handicapped to the village medical practice, which housed three young doctors. Sela called upon many fellow villagers with horse and buggy to provide her with a schedule for just these errands. She loved giving to the town and her volunteer work for the community was endless. Even though she was now a full-time mother, she still helped out with different functions whenever possible. Whether it was a bake sale or a holiday fair, Sela could be counted on. When she was busy helping out she always brought Rutherford along. Little Rutherford who now was a toddler really never bothered anyone.

All the child liked to do was nap. Hours upon endless hours he would find a quiet spot and nestle up to something and close his eyes. The need for parental supervision in Rutherford's case didn't exist. Most of the time wherever they placed him he had dozed off within minutes. Exactly where they placed him is where they would find him many hours later. Rutherford liked to sleep and no on could deny him of his precious need to do so. Only one person would try to change that many years later.

◆

As the years flew by from one decade to the next not much changed for Rutherford who was now a young man. At three foot five inches tall, he was indeed the shortest person in Rutherford. Barker had recently been given the lifetime Mayor award, enabling him to stay in his position for as long as he wanted. Sela still helped in every charity she could. And poor Rutherford could barely keep his eyes open to make it through a day.

As a small child this became an issue of his capability to attend school. For all the grades from kindergarten straight through his senior year, Rutherford found it extremely hard to keep up with the others. The teachers throughout the years found it frustrating to try to teach someone who basically napped through their lessons in class. Rutherford was forced to stay after class for most of his schooling years to keep his grades up. Knowing that this was a problem but never confronting Rutherford's parents on the matter didn't help the situation. Each teacher throughout all Rutherford's grades held the highest regard for Barker and Sela who both had done so much for the town. Most villagers felt that his parents alone had developed the town into the financial success it was. This was the main reason that most teachers tolerated his condition and allowed to pass him each year. Recess was spent alone for Rutherford for his much needed nap and after school play dates never materialized because he'd rather spend the time relaxing rather than playing with his peers. Rutherford spent a lot of time by himself choosing to be alone to sleep rather then force himself to stay alert to make conversation. Now as a young adult he truly was without a friend. His parents made it a point to keep him in their social circle whenever possible, but with their hectic lives, he was more often than not left alone.

Barker and Sela still adored, cherished and worshipped Rutherford and over the years still never discussed his height or the unusual large amount of sleep he required. Rumors could be overheard on occasion from villagers looking to gossip about Rutherford, but were mostly cut short by the loyalty most shared regarding his parents. A loyalty that would be strong for the town of Rutherford, but not much longer for the young man known as Rutherford.

◆

Rutherford was now a man in his twenties unable to hold down a respectable job within the town. Since his parents were considered influential to most in the large village offers for employment for Rutherford were plenty. The only element lacking was his performance on the job. Every simple task he was given was burdened by his desire to sleep in place of his productivity. Each opportunity to succeed diminished as his need for rest increased as he aged. Barker his father had called in most every favor ever promised to him and Sela, too, had exhausted her contacts. Rutherford held many jobs but none for very long. Most times he was either let go for reasons that wouldn't upset his parents or just replaced. For example, when Rutherford was the crossing guard and frequently fell asleep at the side of the road while the children crossed the streets by themselves he caused great concern among the parents, for the safety of their children they had him replaced. As the letter carrier he had kept this job for little over six months until everyone complained about not getting his or her mail delivered in a timely fashion. When the postmaster followed him for a week he learned that Rutherford slept more in the carriage than on the streets delivering mail. People didn't get their mail until early evening causing a commotion in the post office that led to his once again being replaced with an excuse suitable to his parent's understanding. Barker and Sela's understanding was wearing thin but neither of them would ever display any annoyance with their beloved son. They promised to take care of him regardless of any obstacles that crossed their paths. A path that would soon lead them to a trail they never anticipated.

◆

Rutherford had many opportunities in his town for which he was very grateful.

His inability to stay awake and his constant lack of alertness prevented him from earning a steady income within the village. He had been living off the kindness of his parents for the last year or so. Rutherford was restless and needed to work if only to keep himself busy when he wasn't sleeping. One sunny afternoon, Rutherford walked through the busy town stopping at each store he came across and inquired about employment. As he approached each storefront the shopkeepers gave him one excuse after another for not hiring him. The shopkeepers had known of his past history for losing one job after another and feared the outcome would be inevitable at their establishment too. Owners greeted Rutherford in their usual friendly manner wishing him luck as they sent him off requesting he say hello to his folks in the process. Rutherford had the reputation as being non-productive and lazier than any other worker in the village. Rutherford felt defeated and started to head home. His disappointment was no surprise as he was aware that most of the town knew about his sleep disorder. He really had no control over his inability to remain awake and soon the terrible consequences of this would be felt.

◆

Rutherford walked the few short blocks to the corner of Main Street. He turned the corner and was about to head the two blocks to his house when he spotted a help-wanted sign taped to the inside window of the candle factory. Oddly, Rutherford didn't remember seeing the sign when he first walked up the street to start his search for work. Rutherford stepped back to admire the three-story wood building that towered over the other buildings in town. Most other storefronts were a single-story with an occasional two-story building here and there. The candle factory was by far the tallest in town.

The building had three large windows on each level all placed feet apart from one another. The other two floors were designed to match the unique façade of the first floor.

The candle factory sat on the corner of Main Street and took up what was equivalent to three or more other shops on the block. Rutherford had known the owner named Inga.

Inga was in her mid-forties with brown hair and very deep dark brown eyes. She was what most in town called pleasantly plump with a cheerful disposition. Barker and Sela in conversation would refer to her as the town spinster, since she had never married and chances are she wouldn't. When confronted by Inga most people found her pleasant to be with. Her hearty laugh was infectious and her fits of giddiness cheered up even the most depressed individual.

There were three other employees who worked for her in the candle factory that Rutherford also knew by name through purchasing candles he used in his home.

Inga's father had passed down the business to her when he was too sick to continue making the various wax candles. Inga supplied the three surrounding towns with candles in different shapes and sizes and she, too, had one of the most lucrative businesses in the village. But all that was about to change. Her business was going to take off, but this time in a totally different direction.

◆

Hesitantly, Rutherford approached the front door of the candle factory and walked in as he had done so often as a customer. Inga was seated behind the counter helping someone choose between a long and short candle. When she spotted Rutherford, she immediately greeted him in her usual manner.

"Well, Hello Rutherford, weren't you just in here last week? With all those candles you purchased you should be stocked for months." Before she let him reply she knew exactly why he had walked in asking, "It's about the help-wanted sign I posted just a few minutes ago, isn't it? Boy, word of mouth spreads fast in this town, don't you agree?"

Neither denying that was the case or wasn't, she continued, "Well, come on over and lets talk. Give me a minute to finish up with Thula and you and I can chat."

Thula, a frequent customer in the candle store, couldn't resist a comment, "Really, Inga, with all the chatting you do, it amazes me you get any work done in here."

Inga knew that Thula was joking but confirmed her statement, "If you can't have fun in this short thing called life, then when can you?"

Thula nodded in agreement, paid for her purchase, and left the store leaving Rutherford alone with Inga.

"Come, come sit down and tell me why you'd want to work for someone like me, who according to Thula, is the town chatterbox," Inga asked laughing heartily. Rutherford, like most others in the village, found her laughter contagious and giggled along before replying,

" Well, yea, that's why I'm here. Are you looking for someone to start right away? I haven't had a job in quite some time and can start tomorrow if you need me to."

Rutherford then raised his arms straight over his head yawning in his usual manner. Over the many years that was a habit he was known to have had. Rutherford constantly yawned, especially when he was tired. Inga knowing his reputation over the years when it came to work, found herself yawning along with him. She really did like Rutherford and adored his parents as well. Inga, also, believed the success of the town was largely due in part to his parents. Inga, like all Rutherford's former employers, figured she owed Rutherford the chance to prove himself once again. Besides, if she ever needed a favor she would have the Mayor to turn to. She covered her mouth and answered Rutherford's question about the urgency of the position saying, "Old man Jackson decided to retire. Seventy- five years old and he wants to call it quits. Can you imagine? After working for my father for fifty some-odd years and now he wants to fish down at the old mill pond. Guess, he deserves it. Thought I'd have him until he was a hundred. Selfish of me isn't it? Inga watched Rutherford continue to yawn and continued, "Are you tired Rutherford? All that yawning wants to make me take a break and put my head down."

Rutherford tried in vain to wake himself up and look as alert as possible before replying, "Sorry, Inga. It's a bad habit I have. I'm wide-awake, honest. But I really could use the job. It would be nice to be able to earn an income again. It's been so long. But I guess you also know that I haven't been too lucky in the past with some of my other jobs. I promise whatever it is you need me to do, I can do it. Let old man Jackson retire and give me the opportunity to do his job. Thinking about it, what does he actually do? I never see him here when I come into the store."

"Old man Jackson works the night shift. From ten o'clock until six in the morning. He is my candle tester. He tests the amount of time it will take for a candle to burn out. He records the exact time he lights the candles that need to be tested and waits until they burn completely through. He records that time too and then figures out its life. Then he jots down all the information for me to review the following morning. A simple task when you think of it. Doesn't pay much, but it's something when you need work. Besides, it's important that we constantly try new products and also to develop candles that will burn longer and longer. Our customers come from miles and miles away to buy my father's candles. We have to keep coming up with new ideas. Some customers want small squatty ones, others want long thin ones to fit in their candlesticks and now others even want scented ones. Did you ever hear of such a thing? A candle that throws off a pretty aroma when you light it. What will they think up next?" Inga said smiling as she finished.

Rutherford listened to her go on and on about her candles not really caring except for the fact that he needed work desperately. He waited until she finished and in a voice with urgency said, "I'll take it! I mean if you want me that is. Sounds simple enough for me. When can I start?"

Inga sensing his plea for employment and considering the risk of him once again failing, decided to be fair and hire him. After all, old man Jackson had been threatening her in a friendly manner that he really did want to stop working. She had been trying to persuade him to stay on and knew that he wouldn't, forcing her to put the help-wanted sign in her window. Before she told him he had the position, she watched Rutherford for the second time in less than ten minutes stretch and yawn again. In all years she had never seen someone who looked so tired all the time. No, more like Dozzey. Inga confirmed her thought. Yes, DOZZEY, that's what Rutherford was! And from that point on, that was what she would call him.

◆

Barker and Sela were pleased with the news that Rutherford was working in the candle factory. Barker admired Inga and the business sense she had in running such a successful establishment. Sela, however, pitied the long hours Inga put in at the factory preventing her from ever settling down. Sela figured being the town spinster must hurt Inga's feelings but it never showed in her emotions. Inga, regardless of her huge frame, was one of the nicest people in the village of Rutherford surprising both Barker and Sela that she hadn't a fine suitor. Grateful to Inga for hiring Rutherford, both of them went out of their way to stop by the factory and strike up a conversation with her more often than they used to. Inga did have a tendency to chat for hours at a sitting, but for Rutherford's gainful employment they would make the sacrifice on occasion. The candle factory was only two blocks from their house. Before their hectic schedules, they could certainly squeeze in a few minutes to pay a visit to the store. Little did they both know just how little time the store had left.

◆

Rutherford loved his new job. Inga seemed pleased with his performance as well. It would be a year to the day this evening at midnight and Rutherford still held his job. A new record for him. The longest job to date. During the day he now found it easier to sleep, making him capable of staying awake for the night shift.

Inga, always in a good mood, greeted him as he entered the factory for his shift that evening.

Pleased to see Rutherford, Inga asked, "And do you know what today is? At precisely or I should say at the stroke of midnight, it will be one year since I hired you. And who would of thought you could last that…" Inga stopped before saying a word that she knew would hurt him, caught herself and continued, "Anyhow that's water under the bridge. We need to talk about getting you more money."

Rutherford knew what she was implying before she changed the subject and decided to drop it as well excitedly said, "You mean a raise! I never had a raise in my salary before. I never held a job this long either. How much more? I mean when does it start?"

Inga laughed in her fool-hearted way answering, "Whoa, slow down there Dozzey.

In time. How about in your next week's pay? Is that soon enough?"

Delighted, Rutherford thanked her, "Inga, you're the best! I have been so fortunate to work for you. I hope I can outlast old man Jackson and be here for sixty-some odd years."

Inga smiled and reassured Dozzey, "Maybe seventy if you continue the way you have been. Now go scoot upstairs. I have twice the amount of candles for you test. Remember, we have that big order to fill for the McReynolds family. They send their eldest boy from two towns over and stock up on at least a six-month supply. Now go on Dozzey and get busy."

Rutherford looked at her before heading up to the third floor attic where they tested the candles. Before he did so he stretched and yawned for what seemed like minutes.

Inga yelled after him that she would be leaving momentarily and that she would lock the front door. She also noticed Dozzey yawn for the one-thousandth time.

As she was closing the front door, she screamed up to Dozzey what she knew he would hear.

"And remember Dozzey, no sleeping on the job," giggling as she pulled the door shut.

Inga had said this on several occasions over the last year and it was now a joke between the two of them. A joke that would soon be anything but funny.

◆

Rutherford had placed the thirty candles all around the room on the tables set up for testing. One by one he lit each candle and wrote down the exact time he did. After the fifteen minutes it took to light each candle, Rutherford went to sit by the large grandfather clock that he watched until the first candle burned out. From the large grandfather clock he recorded all his time. It was almost ten-thirty. Usually at eleven o'clock, Rutherford would have a bite to eat. Nothing fancy, just a sandwich and piece of fruit his mother had packed for him in a brown paper bag. Afterwards, he would play solitaire with the deck of cards old man Jackson had left behind. Then once the candles started to burn out the rest of the night would fly by. Between the recording of the time and then cleaning up all the melted wax, six o'clock in the morning was upon him. Tonight, however, felt different for Rutherford. He was excited about his one-year anniversary at the factory and the prospect of a raise. His first raise. Rutherford looked up at the clock. In just four minutes the stroke of midnight would mark his one-year on the job. Rutherford yawned. And then suddenly, he started to feel very, very tired. Rutherford was feeling very sluggish. Extremely sluggish. Rutherford tried to keep his eyes from closing. In less than a minute, the clock would strike midnight. Rutherford needed to rest for a second. He started to panic. He felt like he was under some sort of spell. There were still so many candles that were burning. He couldn't afford to fall asleep on the job. The outcome would be a catastrophe. Rutherford needed fresh air. He decided to go outside for a few seconds to wake himself up. Rutherford looked at the clock as it chimed to the stroke of midnight. He'd be back in less than a minute. Rutherford headed to the stairs leading down two flights to the first floor. As he dragged his body to the stairwell, he accidentally bumped into a chair. The chair swayed from side to side before it finally tipped over as he made his way down the steps. Rutherford never realized that he had bumped into the chair. He was too exhausted to even keep his eyes open. The chair tilted into one of the many tables that held the burning candles. Two of the candles fell over igniting the table at once. Flames from the first wood table spread rapidly to the next table and from one table to the next. Soon the whole third floor was up in flames.

Rutherford was oblivious to the fire on the third floor. He was grateful that he had somehow made it out of the factory while he was still awake. What he didn't realize as the third floor fire now engulfed the second floor, was that he had fallen fast asleep at the curb. It wasn't until moments later among the many screams from the townspeople that had fled their houses and now ran up and down the streets, was just how he wished he could have slept forever.

◆

Luckily for what remained of the town of Rutherford there was a passing thunderstorm that opened the skies to a heavy downpour the night the infamous fire ruined their village. As it ended up, two-thirds of the town went up in flames before the heavy rains extinguished the flames. Main Street no longer existed since all the attached businesses had burned down to the ground. Fortunately, no lives were lost due to the speedy response of the volunteer men within the village firehouse. While most villagers scrambled to safety with their families, many other villagers pitched in to try to stop the fiercely spreading fire to no avail. Many volunteers were able to evacuate the townspeople that still slept before fires engulfed their homes. Barker Baccus, the Mayor, accessed the damage. After much careful consideration and hardship he assured the people of Rutherford that the village could be salvaged. They all would rebuild the damage and start anew. He would back the town he was so proud of that he named his only son after it. Many refused to believe his ideas of rebuilding the town and chose to move on to another town with what little belongings they had left. Inga, the candle factory owner, was most furious. It was her stupidity in hiring Dozzey that caused the eventual destruction to what remained of the town of Rutherford. She demanded action to be taken against Dozzey and his poor judgment. Inga was so persistent that she soon had many followers who also wanted justice for Rutherford's crucial mistake. Barker, being the Mayor wanted his son to stand a fair trial. Two days after the fire, they held a town meeting in the Town Square to hear what had happened on that disastrous night. Rutherford, backed by his parents, shakily took the stand, as hundreds watched and retold his fateful tale. He tried to plead that some sort of spell was cast on him causing him to feel more exhausted than ever. Villagers looked on in pity and some with anger, but it was Inga who spoke out with feelings of hatred, "Dozzey, that's what I would call him!' Her voice grew louder as she continued, "All I did was give this sorry excuse of a man, a very little man need I remind all of you, a chance to redeem himself. And what does Dozzey do, just that, sleeps while our whole village burns to the ground."

The crowd started to get angry and restless while even a few shouts of obscenities were heard from the back, urging Barker to speak up on behalf of his son before a riot would break out.

"Now hold on Inga," Barker stepped in front of his son. Rutherford didn't start the fire himself. No one knows for sure what exactly did happen. Why blame my son when we don't have any evidence proving his guilt."

"Guilty! We don't need any evidence. His carelessness in even leaving the factory in the first place proves his guilt. What more proof do we need? My poor father, may he rest in peace, who started this business so many years ago and to think by one stupid act from an individual who is known and has been for years to fall asleep on EVERY job. What more proof do you need?" Inga rebutted.

"I say he should pay dearly for this. Look at what he did to OUR town! What do you say we take justice into our OWN hands?" Inga shouted.

The crowd started to push its way up to the platform that Barker, Sela and Rutherford stood on.

Sela could stand it no longer and she, too, feared for her son's life. Sela looked at all the faces in the crowd. Many were people she had helped in one way or another. She felt sorry for them all, but Barker and herself had also lost their modest home to the fire. Their house was only two blocks away and the intensity of the spreading fire consumed their home within the first half hour. The only homes left standing were the houses and farms that were on the perimeter of the village.

Sela focused on the people she knew she could make an appeal to and spoke in her most soft-spoken voice, "Please, I beg all of you, THIS was an accident. Surely you can't think Rutherford would deliberately do this to OUR town. Look at everything my husband and I have done for this town. For us, don't do this, please. Please spare my only child any suffering. Haven't we all suffered enough?"

No longer the Merry person she once was or appeared to be, Inga knew she had the attention of the angry crowd, "We don't want you, missus. We aren't looking to do you or your husband any harm. We wouldn't have anything to show if it weren't for you two.

But Dozzey must pay! He doesn't deserve to rebuild with the few of us willing to stay on.

Dozzey must go!" Inga started to chant the expression over and over before the angry crowd joined in. The noise level in the crowd became unbearable. Barker, not only the Mayor, but also Rutherford's father knew they would have no choice. His son committed the worst possible act to the town of Rutherford and Barker knew he would never be forgiven. Nothing he or his wife could say or plead would convince the crowd to leave Rutherford alone. He did what he knew he must, not as his father, but as the Mayor of the village. He turned to the crowd and his sternest voice said, "As the Mayor of this village I will not tolerate any violence to this human being. What he did was an accident, of that I am sure. But I do know that this village will never be the same if he stays among us. So it is my intention to banish Rutherford from our village for good."

Sela almost passed out from what she had just heard. Her own husband and father of her only child just banished him from the village. But as she looked around at the crowd who seemed pleased by this last statement, she also knew in her heart that this was the only way to save their only son. Barker and Sela hugged their son with both their arms tightly wrapped around him and whispered 'I love you back and forth to one another. The scene was heart wrenching to those who cared to see. Not many did.

Only moments before, the crowd that was stirring with rage now seemed satisfied with the answer to the problem. They started applauding and were now cheering, as they knew that they had won. Rutherford was banished with no option to return. He must leave right away. Before the following morning. Barker and Sela agreed to this request knowing they had both saved their son from a much worse fate. They, however, would stay on and once again rebuild the ruined village. They owed the town that much for their son's mistake. Even if it weren't his entire fault. Life without Rutherford would never be the same for them. This pained them both. But, for those who were willing to rebuild, they no longer feared having to look at Rutherford again. The chants were deafening. Inga seemed the most pleased and now stood up on the platform alongside the Baccus family. She stared into Dozzey's eyes and said, "If only you hadn't fallen asleep on the job Dozzey, none of this would have happened. But you did, and you can't turn the clock back. You got lucky thanks to your folks. If I had my way I would have nailed you to a cross. Count your blessings Dozzey and leave right away."

Inga took over on the podium and watched as Barker, Sela and Dozzey left the towns square for the precious few hours they would have together. She was in control now.

Inga, who now was more spiteful and bitter, knew she would rebuild her father's legacy and this time make it the best candle factory in the country. She spoke to the crowd about her future as well as theirs and in less than twenty minutes the now quieted crowd left to see the ruins of their village.

And in less than six hours, right before midnight, Rutherford said his final goodbye to his most beloved parents and fled into the night and off to the Black Forest.

8

Cranky and Emdee sensed that immediate danger was in store for the whole group. First Emdee, then Cranky and now Dozzey were all hypnotized in some sort of trance. Emdee was the one to realize that something wasn't right when he watched Cranky and now Dozzey both follow in his footsteps. The three of them stopped by the foot of their beds and had distant memories that neither of them was willing to share. Emdee grabbed Dozzey and whisked him away from his bed, shaking him out of whatever evil grip had its hold on him. Dozzey, of course, stretched and yawned and pleaded to sleep. He fell to the floor and had to be picked up by both Cranky and Emdee. They dragged him while he slept over to the landing but not before Merry had made his way over to his bed. Merry no longer looked Merry. A look of terror replaced his cheerful face alerting both Emdee and Cranky that it was too late. He was transfixed in fear. All Emdee could say as he held back the others was, "Here we go again…"

Whitaker Gump

Cheerful, joyful, this little man is very,
So he shall be given the name of MERRY...

-Gaston

9

Way, way back in a quiet village the birth of a miniature baby occurred. Given the name of Whitaker Gump by his mother Gwen, after his late father, who had passed away from a carriage accident in their village months prior to his birth. Gwen Gump, her mother Genneva, Whitaker's grandmother, raised the baby on their own. The small house they lived in was in the center of the town of Smirn Oaks. Needing a more steady income, Whitaker senior had moved Gwen back to her hometown two years after they were married. Employment and the fact that Gwen wanted to be closer to her mother and father were the key factors in their decision. Work was plentiful in the much larger town and they were expecting their first child. A wise decision considering Gwen's father had passed away from a sudden heart attack shortly, thereafter; right before any of their children were born. The first couple of years after the death of Gwen's father were truly hard. Whitaker worked at the stable breeding and tending horses, and then tragedy struck again. It was there at his job just three months before the birth of his fourth child that the accident occurred. While he was harnessing an aggressive horse to a buggy, the horse reins had gotten entangled around Whitaker. The horse took off dragging him under the wheels of the buggy through the streets of Smirn Oaks as onlookers watched in horror, unable to help. The horse finally stopped down at the riverbank to drink. By then, Whitaker had suffered many bruises and broken bones to his face and body. Not quite a week later despite being under the constant supervision and care of the town doctor, Whitaker died from his injuries. The news was devastating to Gwen who was pregnant with her fourth child. Her mother, Genneva, supported her through the whole horrifying experience. The town's residents also donated money to help with the expenses in response to the two tragedies that were bestowed upon the men in the family. A rather large collection was taken up throughout the town. Many families, sympathizing with their pain and loss, were very generous both financially and spiritually to the two remaining women. A large donation was made. The only Church in town also took part of their yearly tithes to help the family of women get by. Genneva and Gwen accepted all the contributions and were thankful to the village inhabitants. Gwen's parents were very respected in the town that they had lived in for so many years so the villagers were more than willing to help out. Gwen would have probably lost her fourth child just from the stress alone, but her mother made her keep up her strength for the sake of her other children. Her three young daughters, all under the age of six, were also traumatized with the loss of their loving, doting father. Gwen had to be strong for them and needed to keep all their spirits up. Then the miracle occurred. Gwen had given birth to a baby boy. A very tiny baby boy. Gwen didn't care that he was so puny. A boy to carry on the family name. Whitaker junior was the last of the four Gump children. Bliss, Joy, and Glee were his three older sisters. The three girls were delighted to have a baby brother and fought among themselves just to take care of him. In a household of five females each one adored Whitaker more than the next. There wasn't a time when one of his sisters or either of the two adult women weren't fussing over him. As he became a toddler, he still remained tiny. To most of the other villagers they expressed concern whenever they came upon him as he was pushed through the village by one of the five females in the house. The five Gump females couldn't care less. They were so proud of little Whitaker. He was such a beautiful boy. Regardless of his very small frame, they all continued to adore him. Any one and certainly no one could put him down or make a comment without getting a long-winded lecture from one of the five Gump females. The five females watched his every move and protected him from any snickers made about his height. Whitaker may have not grown in size as he became a young boy but his personality made up for this. Ever since he was a baby he smiled constantly. His mother found this peculiar for an infant not to cry from gas pains, dirty diapers, and even teething as he continued to grow. Her three daughters had been quite a handful and had required much attention when they each had fits of crying. Bliss and Glee didn't sleep through the night until they were each six months old. Whitaker, however, was sleeping straight through the night within the first week. Every morning his temperament was more and more cheerful. From early morning to late in the evening, Whitaker was a healthy bouncing baby boy. His smile radiated from cheek-to-cheek causing anyone to glance at him to automatically smile in return. In spite of his shortness, as Whitaker grew older the town ignored this fact and treated him like any other. His jovial nature by far outweighed his appearance causing most villagers to laugh along with him. Throughout his early years in school even his classmates found him to be most likable. Whitaker had all the qualities of a truly elated individual. Among his peers he was the class clown, which even the teacher found amusing and joined in much of the laughter. The town of Smirn Oaks became a wonderful place to live. The villagers gave credit to Whitaker for always having a smile on his face wherever he was seen. His smile tended to spread among all who came across him. This delighted his mother and grandmother who were now held in high regard for raising such a delightful young man. His sisters, Bliss, Joy and Glee also shined among their fellow villagers due to Whitaker's constant cheerfulness. It was their love and kindness in helping to raise Whitaker that made him the man that he was. A man who later on would be anything but that. A man who would cross paths with a very unhappy man.

◆

Gaston came to the town of Smirn Oaks for the sole purpose of finding a young maiden to wed and bring back with him to his farm many miles away. With his strapping build he stood tall at six foot four with a full head of jet-black hair and the most beautiful dazzling blue eyes. He was a lumberjack by trade and a burly man at that. When Gaston first walked through the streets of Smirn Oaks, the women were mesmerized by his good looks. Gaston paid most of the young women no mind. He had searched many of the surrounding towns looking for the right woman with which to share his life. He knew what he wanted and he wouldn't settle for anything less than perfect. Upon first setting eyes on Glee Gump, he knew that it was love at first sight. Glee was of a slender build no more than five foot two with blue eyes and blond hair. Her hair was long and straight and blew in the wind as she walked. Gaston had to meet her. He followed her for three blocks until she eventually stopped and entered a shop called Gumps Galore. Gaston caught up to her and finally stopped in front of the shop as well. Gaston peeked inside the large storefront window and saw what appeared to be wedding gowns and men's tuxedos. He assumed it was some type of boutique that specialized in brides and grooms. Glee went around the counter to join two other girls of dazzling beauty. Gaston, keeping out of sight, watched her help around the store tending to customers who had entered.

He found it very amusing that she would work in such a place. He stood there for the next twenty-five minutes gaping at her beauty. Gaston was too nervous to approach her in front of the other two women who worked in the store. He would wait for her to leave and then walk up alongside her and strike up a conversation. Satisfied that he knew what he was doing he turned to cross the street. He also realized at that moment that this would be the girl he would marry. The one woman he would spend his life with.

However, what he didn't realize was the short man who also worked there as the tailor was her brother. A brother who could never be his brother-in-law just because of his size.

◆

"Whitaker, are you almost done with Mr. Hoppins? There are two more fittings for tuxes and we'll be closing soon," Bliss yelled from behind the counter. Gumps Galore was a bridal shop established by the three Gump sisters. They all had a taste for fashion etiquette and wanted to put their designs to use. So with the help from their yearly donations from the local church, Gwen and her mother helped get them started.

They found an old store that had closed up years before and bargained with the landlord to let them rent it at an affordable price. The landlord, knowing their situation, gave in and the store became one of the most successful businesses in town. Men and women from three towns over came to buy their gowns and tuxedos. Compliments by word of mouth and the merchandise considered elegant, had people bustling from all over just to make a purchase. Bliss, Joy and Glee each patterned their own designs. From the stencils they took the material and made them into dresses. Whitaker had a knack for men's fashion, because he lived with all women and designed the tuxedos. He tailored the men who came into the store and fitted them with just the right tux. His height sometimes made it difficult to reach the taller men who came in but with the help of a stepstool he was capable of measuring any man no matter how tall.

So together the four of them created a lucrative business in the first two years alone. Now their financial success allowed them to payback and contribute rather large donations to the Church and other charitable organizations.

"In a minute, Bliss. Mr. Hoppins is a large man who needs that extra touch. Just tell the others I'll be right with them. Don't worry about closing the store. I can take care of that," Whitaker said in his usual note of sunshine.

"Really, Bliss, Whitaker can handle closing up. He does that at least two nights a week.

If all he has left is two more fittings, then we can leave and let him finish up," Joy stated.

Glee also felt the same way and agreed, "I don't know about you girls, but I'm very tired.

Would you mind if I left a little earlier? I have a splitting headache."

Both her sisters nodded an okay. The workload was divided up equally and under situations such as this could be handled accordingly. None of the four Gump children were jealous or resentful of one another. If one of them needed time off they rearranged their schedules to meet the other's needs. The shop would be closing soon so Glee knew they wouldn't mind. She quickly thanked her two sisters, Bliss and Joy, and waved a fast goodbye to Whitaker and was out the door.

No sooner did she leave the store, than she was approached by Gaston. He walked up to her and with his charmingly good looks and persuasive personality swept her off her feet.

Glee had met her Mr. Right. It was only a matter of time before she would realize just how wrong he really was.

◆

The next couple of weeks the courtship was enchanting for Glee. Secretly she would meet Gaston, who now rented a one room flat in town to be close to her, and the two of them fell madly in love with one another. Being the youngest of the three girls, Glee felt like she was the one who should marry last. It was never her intention to fall in love so fast. Gaston was a true gentleman. Her desire now was to marry this fine young man, but only with her family's blessings. She no longer could keep Gaston a secret. Glee had to introduce this wonderful man to her family. A family that everyone loved. A family she knew he would love. That was until Gaston would meet Whitaker.

◆

The day had finally arrived for the introductions to take place. Gaston knew Glee had two sisters and a brother in addition to her mother and grandmother. He had never met any of them and had only seen her two sisters from afar. He was anxious to meet them all. Glee had arranged for her mother Gwen and her grandmother to come to the shop for a surprise. When it was just about closing time the five Gump women and one Gump man were sitting inside the shop for the unexplained event. Glee told them to dress nicely as they would all go out for a special dinner afterwards. Sensing the overwhelming elation from Glee, the whole family waited for the surprise with bated breath. When the door finally opened and the bells chimed that hung over the door all six sets of eyes focused on the most handsome man they had ever seen. Glee jumped to her feet and ran up to greet the man she so loved. As she went into hellos and introductions she never noticed where Gaston's eyes really were focused. She was too busy showing off her most prized possession.

As Gaston made his way from one woman of the family to the next, his eyes never left the one thing he knew he could never really embrace. He prayed this small thing in front of him was not her brother. The man was so tiny in comparison to his family.

With a full white beard and round plump shape this little person was no taller than three foot something. Gaston knew that the introduction to this short man was inevitable. Glee lit up when she came to Whitaker. She was so delighted to introduce her most beloved brother to the man of her dreams. As Glee introduced Whitaker to Gaston, she immediately sensed Gaston tense. Making up for his discomfort she continued to praise her youngest brother. Gaston now stepped back and resisted the hand that stood out in front of him. Gaston was frozen in place and watched in horror as this little man reached up for a handshake. What came out of Gaston's mouth next would change Glee's feeling for him forever.

◆

"And just what are you? I'm sorry. I mean how come you are so small? No... That's not right either. What I meant to say is that your sisters are so beautiful and you... You are so..." Gaston was babbling like a nervous fool. All five females of the Gump family stood there staring in disbelief at what they were hearing. Whitaker sensing the tension that was now mounting decided to break the silence and in his usual manner said, " Well, very nice to meet you! Indeed it is a pleasure on my behalf to finally meet the man Glee has spoken so highly of these past few days." Whitaker put his hand down at his side knowing that Gaston would never shake it. He also knew that he would have to patch things up and fast if harmony and peace were to continue in this first meeting.

"So, Gaston, Glee tells us that you are planning a surprise for all of us and wanted to have us all gathered together before you stated it. So, please go on and tell us," Whitaker continued. Gaston didn't move and couldn't speak. For a full minute no one spoke. All the eyes were now on Whitaker. Gaston was still in shock at this little being and how he came to be. Nothing attractive or appealing graced this tiny individual and it appalled him to be in his presence.

Waiting for what seemed like a lifetime but was no more than a full minute, Glee finally put an end to all the silence, "Sorry to have gathered you all here today. Whatever Gaston had to say can wait. Actually, it Will have to wait. All of a sudden I don't feel so well and if you would all excuse me I have to...." Overwhelmed by her emotions, Glee suddenly turned away from them all and ran briskly toward the door. Glee left everyone still shaken up over what they all just witnessed. Gaston turned and left without so much as a goodbye in pursuit of his future bride-to-be. A future bride-to-be that would never fill that role.

◆

Gaston, over the course of several weeks, tried in vain to persuade Glee to forgive him.

He desperately tried every attempt to seek her forgiveness with no such luck. Glee could never ever forget the disgusted look that came over Gaston's face when he first set eyes on Whitaker. Whitaker who was their lifeline to overcome any obstacles with just a simple note of kindness. Whitaker who didn't have a mean bone in his body. Glee listened to Gaston plead with her to give him another chance. He wanted to elope with no fancy wedding like they had originally discussed. All that had since changed when Gaston had met her brother. Glee couldn't understand why Gaston wasn't even willing to let Whitaker into his world. Their future world. Every time Glee had brought up or even mentioned Whitaker's name, Gaston quickly changed the subject. Gaston had a new plan of action. Together, they would ride off into the sunset. Just the two of them. Once they were married they would start a new family of their own. Glee knew his plan would never include her old family. Gaston had no intention of coming back to town once she was his new wife. Glee could never leave her family. After all, family was all she ever had.

◆

As the weeks passed so did any chance of reconciling with the woman he loved and was meant to spend his life with. Gaston couldn't convince Glee of the perfect life he could give her. Every time, the conversation would always lead back to Whitaker.

Gaston now came to despise the mention of his name. Glee sensed this from him and would no longer even glance in his direction. Once Glee had told him she had fallen out of love with him, he knew their relationship was doomed. Gaston would have to move on as much as he didn't want to without Glee. The last few days were the hardest for Gaston. He now realized that his future with Glee was no longer an option. As long as he could never accept Whitaker, Glee wouldn't be part of his life. Gaston hated the misfit and wanted nothing more than to seek revenge of Whitaker. He had never meant such an individual as cheerful as he. Most men were anything but that optimistic, which now in his case proved right. Whitaker was just so darn pleasant and agreeable that all at once Gaston put a name to his sunny disposition. A name that fit Whitaker and his positive attitude all the time. Gaston would forever call him MERRY. And with that thought, Gaston knew just how the name of Merry could change Whitaker forever. Gaston was pleased with the idea that popped into his head and started to head over in the direction of Gumps Galore. He would wait until the three sisters left for the evening, which they had done on several occasions leaving Whitaker by himself to close up the store. If it took a couple of days for this to happen, Gaston would wait patiently. After he was certain Whitaker was alone Gaston would stage his best performance to date. An act that only Gaston knew he would be able to pull off. An act of revenge so sweet that only he could taste it.

◆

Gaston waited until the last customer exited the store. He had watched the shop for the last three days and his opportunity had now come. Making certain no other customers would enter he waited across the street hidden out of view behind a tree. And as he had suspected, Whitaker was closing up for the night. There were still plenty of hours of daylight left until dark and Gaston still had much to do. He slowly crossed the street and walked up to Whitaker just as he was locking up the door. Startled, Whitaker turned to face him before saying, "Gaston, what a pleasure to see you. I thought you already left town. Sorry, but you just missed Glee. Glee is already gone for the evening. By the way, I'm so sorry that things didn't work out for you two." Whitaker never did find out the real reason for their split. Every time he asked Glee she would tell him it just wasn't meant to be. Whitaker knew he was part if not all the reason for the relationship to break up. No one else in the family would confirm or deny this statement whenever he questioned them. Since that was the case he no longer assumed anything differently. He had not seen hide nor hair of Gaston since that awkward night many weeks before. Whitaker was hesitant to continue conversation but in his good nature asked, "So, there is no reason to wait around here, Glee is gone until morning." Repeating what his sister told him time and time again and hoping to ease the pain that still clearly showed on Gaston's face Whitaker said, "I guess it just wasn't meant to be."

Gaston couldn't believe what this disgusting little creature had just said. Keeping composed, Gaston had to speak slowly as to not show any disgust in his voice answering, "I'm not here to see her. I know it's over. Glee didn't want me back and I guess I'll have to live with that. I'm leaving Smirn Oaks for another town and a chance for a new bride.

I was hoping to purchase a last-minute tuxedo to take with me when I leave. I know you were closing up shop but I was hoping you could squeeze me in for old time's sake. What do you say, Merry?"

Whitaker thought he heard Gaston just call him Merry. Confused, he asked, "Did you just call me Merry or am I hearing things?"

Gaston knew he almost blew it and covered up for his slip of the tongue by doing what he did best. Gaston changed the subject and in less than two minutes had Merry opening the door to the shop to fit him for a tuxedo. A tuxedo he would not use for some time. After all, a woman like Glee was not easy to find. As Gaston followed Merry into the back room to be fitted for his tuxedo, he smiled. His plan would be in effect in just a matter of a few minutes. And poor little Merry would never be looked at by his family of women or from any of the other townspeople for that matter. Glee constantly reminded him of just how well-liked and popular Merry was in the village. The village that would soon cast a new opinion on this little man named Merry. The man that Gaston would convince everyone in the town was gay.

◆

"Come back! Please, Gaston! I didn't touch you there. I would never touch anyone in their privates. Oh, please don't do this. Please!" Panicked, Whitaker was shouting as he ran down the street after Gaston and straight to the Center of the Town Square. Around this time of day the town square was busy with people returning home from their jobs and leisurely strollers enjoying a late afternoon walk. Gaston ran smack in the middle of the square performing his best act and screaming for Merry to keep his distance from him. Gaston was calling him gay. A word that everyone feared. Everyone's head turned to face them. It now made sense when he thought he heard Gaston call him Merry. Gaston knew exactly what he was doing and never had any intention of buying a tuxedo. Gaston came to destroy him just for being small and for ruining his chances with Glee. From the first moment Gaston laid eyes on him, he was repulsed. No one in the town of Smirn Oaks looked at his height as some sort of freakish thing but he sensed with Gaston's persistence it was soon about to change. People now congregated in a circle around Gaston who had now pointed his finger at Merry accusing him of fondling him when he was being fitted for a tuxedo. There were loud gasps among Whitaker's peers as he entered the crowd who separated to let him in. Being Merry was one thing, but being gay was not an acceptable characteristic by any means. No man should have anything or any relations with a man. Gaston knew he had the crowd's attention and looking like he was visibly shaken continued, "He touched me! Grabbed me in my most PRIVATE area! Could you all imagine? All I did was want him to fit me for a tuxedo so I could find a bride. I wanted to look presentable when I did search for a new bride, and HE touched me! This so-called little man who is always so MERRY!" There was silence in the crowd. Everyone was looking at Whitaker in horror.

Whitaker stopped in the center. By now everyone within a two-block radius came to investigate what all the commotion was about. Whitaker spotted his mother Gwen and his three sisters, Bliss, Joy and Glee fast approaching. By then the crowd was up in arms for fear that a gay man now lived in their village. Whitaker tried to plead his innocence as Gaston pretended to be the victim. No one believed Whitaker. It all made sense to them as to why he was indeed always so Merry. Raised by a household of women didn't help. The reason was right there staring the whole town in the face. People started to believe they were touched as well when they were fitted for a tuxedo. Even so, Glee came to his rescue telling everyone that Gaston was trying to pay her back for breaking off their relationship. The crowd didn't care to hear her. What they did care about was that a man in THEIR town was gay and this couldn't be. Until he left the town, the people of Smirn Oaks would never treat any of the Gump family the same again. That was just how small towns were. Whitaker left with his head face down in shame while his mother and three sisters protected him like they had always done in the past. Gaston, too, had left that evening never to show his face in Smirn Oaks again. His work was done. Since Glee had refused his offer to be his bride he would make her pay. The town would never let Merry into their lives again. Just as Glee had shut him out of hers. The only difference was that Gaston would move on whereas Merry had no place else to go.

◆

The following months were miserable for the Gump family. Each member of the Gump females tried to hold meetings to prove their brothers innocence. Not many people cared to show for these meetings since the rumors had spread like wild fire throughout Smirn Oaks of Whitakers preference for men. The Villagers had now chosen to ignore all the members of the Gump family. Until Whitaker told the truth about what really happened when he fondled that burly man by the name of Gaston, no one wanted anything to do with any of the family. Gump's Galore hadn't had a local customer in weeks and if not for the surrounding towns that were still in the dark about the rumors, they would have been forced to close their once successful business. Whitaker feared they would wind up in financial distress once again. He also feared that this time the villagers and even the Church might not be so willing to help out with a supposedly gay man living in their house. To keep the business alive, the sisters arranged for the customers from other towns to come late in the day. They made the appointments almost at dusk to keep them away from the other townspeople. They told the out of town customers that their schedules during regular hours were full and luckily for them no one argued either way about the later than normal appointments. Whitaker was never the same since the incident that changed how people felt about him. He couldn't walk the short distance home without fingers pointed at him and sometimes-nasty names being shouted. Whitaker didn't understand how this could have happened. All he ever wanted to do was spread sunshine and happiness to everyone he came across. He never had any other intentions of anything, especially with another man. But that didn't matter anymore to Whitaker. What mattered most was that his family persevere. And with him in the town that could never be. The Gump females could move on without him, of that he was sure.

What Whitaker feared more than anything else, was that he could not move on without them.

◆

Whitaker knew what he must do. As much as it pained him he could no longer jeopardize his families existence. Keeping up his best cheery disposition that he hadn't shown in weeks, Whitaker prepared a gala feast to celebrate life. No special occasion better than to be Merry for what they had. After filling their bellies with so much good food, Bliss, his oldest sister, played the harmonica while the whole Gump family danced and laughed liked they had done so many times in the past before the incident with Gaston.

Gwen had brought out some wine she had hidden in the cellar for special occasions such as this and they all drank. Even Whitaker's grandmother drank more than usual. The stress on the Gump females was all too much for them. Not one of them would ever turn their backs on Whitaker. He was and always would be their special pride. Whitaker knew it would devastate them all when he did what he knew what he must. He also knew in time they would eventually move on. The Gump women were not to be taken down. Whitaker watched them drink themselves into oblivion. The festivities lasted for hours, which made Whitaker all the happier. He would cherish these memories for a lifetime. After a while one by one the Gump women called it a night. Between the drinking and dancing they would sleep fitfully into the night. Whitaker waited until the last of them was fast asleep. He then kissed each one of them as they slept peacefully in their beds.

Whitaker wrote a detailed letter explaining his reasons for leaving in hopes that one day they would come to forgive him for leaving. He then packed his bag for his journey. He did know that by leaving, his family would be spared and that the town once again would accept them. Suddenly, a tear fell. Then many more tears flowed from his eyes and down his cheeks into his full white beard. Whitaker was crying. Something he had never done before. He would never forget his family. And, as Whitaker made a point to pass each loved-one one more time, he headed out the door and deep into the woods of the Black Forest.

10

"Help me, Cranky. Grab him by the shoulders and pull. When I count to three you pull and I'll push. Ready, one…three, I mean…two... three!" Emdee counted trying to ready both Cranky and himself for the rather large task at hand. "I got em! Now push against his chest and jus maybe he'll snap out of it. Besides Emdee, what's going on up here?" Cranky said as he yanked on Merry's suspenders.

"Some kind of spell is my guess. Look at the others. Yourshyness, Hachew and Toodum look like they're about to faint."

Dozzey who had just moments ago gone through his harrowing experience joined the other two in helping get Merry far away from his bed. As the three of them continued to struggle with Merry, who now was beginning to awaken, a sudden breeze blew open the shutters. A wind whipped through the room blowing the curtains right off their rods. The breeze formed a little dust pile in the center of the room. From a dust pile it formed a small tunnel that looked like a mini tornado right in the middle of the floor. Emdee, Cranky, Dozzey, and now still frightened Merry made their way to the landing with the other three dwarfs. Cranky was the first to notice before pointing out what the others had already noticed too. Yourshyness who had stepped aside to make room for Merry and his rescuers, was pulled into the force of the mini tornado leading him directly to the spot where four of the seven had now been. Yourshyness was standing in front of his bed with his eyes pleading for someone to come and rescue him. But it was too late, the wind had created a barrier too strong for the others to break through. Yourshyness panicked and tried to move but the breeze held him in place as, he too, was gripped with a sudden terror from a long ago past.

Kendall Peterson

*This little man will be given a life afraid
to show his kindness, So he shall be given
the name of YOURSHYNESS...*

-Hanna

11

Somewhere in a village at least several days journey away, a pint-sized infant was born. Kenwood and Delia Peterson took both their names and came up with Kendall for their second son. Noticing right away that their second son at birth was small in comparison to his older brother, Kenrich, they just assumed it to be what the Good Lord chose to give them. Kenrich was just two years old and already larger than most other toddlers his age. Now, having recently moved to the town of Hickabee, Kenwood Peterson replaced the Reverend who had recently retired and moved to be with his widowed sister many miles away. The Reverend and Kenwood had met less than a year ago at a Church function and it was then that the Reverend asked Kenwood to come and reside at the house attached to the only Church for the three surrounding towns. Reverend Halliwell had heard only good things about Kenwood and was eager to have him assume his position as the Pastor of his Church. For Kenwood, having been a Preacher in a much smaller village, the opportunity to spread the word of the Gospel to a much larger town made the move easier for the Petersons. Kenwood's wife, Delia, was known as the Preacher's wife from the moment they moved into their new village. Neighbors and fellow parishioners welcomed them with open arms. The small white house, just outside of town, which was attached to the Church, was freshly painted. Many neighbors pitched in to make the house and property surrounding the Church all the more livable for the new preacher. A white picket fence was also put up for the small children of the Petersons' to keep them safe on their grounds. The villagers were very excited to have new blood in the Church. Retired Reverend Halliwell was much loved in the town but a much younger Pastor was needed to rejuvenate a faithless community.

Over the past ten years, the town of Hickabee had suffered through some difficult times leading many villagers to lose their faith in believing that things would ever get better.

Since the arrival of the Petersons, that was all changing.

In the short time spent in Hickabee, Kenwood's sermons had inspired so many of the few remaining parishioners that word of mouth had quickly spread that Kenwood was truly a gifted individual sent down from the heavens to help redeem all who felt they needed to be. Now, each and every Sunday, the morning service was enjoyed by a Church filled to capacity with many parishioners traveling miles away from other towns to be inspired by the new Pastor. Hickabee was reborn. Businesses that were near bankruptcy had now proven lucrative due to so many outsiders who came to the Church and paid visits after services to the stores within their village. The whole community felt the Petersons were to be thanked for the complete turn around in the town. Kenwood and Delia were held in highest regard wherever they ventured into town. Residents in Hickabee were grateful for their arrival and prayed they would remain with them for a long time to come.

What the Petersons didn't know at that time was that most of the family would stay with the exception of Kendall.

◆

As an infant, Kendall remained very tiny. Kenwood and Delia accepted his petite form and tried to make up for it by paying more attention to Kendall's needs. The results were anything but positive. In fact, the opposite response was received from Kendall. As a baby, whenever his mother or father picked up Kendall, he cried until he was put back in his crib. Both Kenwood and Delia found this somewhat odd but realized that if it worked in keeping little Kenwood quiet then they would let it be. As he became a toddler, he shied away from his parents and even his older brother. Most of the time he preferred to be left alone to play by himself. Kenrich, who was very outgoing and social made up for him. Given any opportunity he loved to be the center of attention, whereas Kendall would rather be hidden in the background. This continued to disturb Kenwood and Delia since the invitations to most villagers' homes were endless. Delia would have to drag Kendall right up to the front porch during their visits and on several occasions found this quite embarrassing when the neighbors and parishioners joined in coaxing him into their homes. Once inside, Kendall would find a corner and basically spend most of the evening hidden there. When supper was placed on the table Kendall would never look up while he was eating and rarely ever spoke or participated in conversations. The awkwardness made the Petersons come up with excuses for turning down offers from their friends. The way Kendall reacted around other individuals made his parents and the company they were visiting very uncomfortable. So the visits became fewer and fewer. Becoming more alarmed, the Petersons took their second son to the town doctor. Doctor Rubenstein said it was nothing to be overly concerned about. Kendall was in excellent health but unfortunately he was also extremely introverted. Considering his height was still rather short could also be a result of his being so timid. Given time the doctor said he should come out of it. When he did grow taller, which his parents so often prayed would happen, then maybe his self-confidence would too. Little did they know that when his baby sister, Daisy, was born six years after him, just how bad Kendall's behavior would become.

◆

Daisy grew and caught up to Kendall in height by her second birthday. Her parents doted on her every whim. Kendall was treated the way he now preferred to be. Alone by himself. With an older son and now a beautiful young daughter, who were of normal height, Kenwood and Delia tended to ignore Kendall. Kendall also had to deal with being the middle child. All these strikes against him did anything but boost his morale. However, whenever the family gathered together for meals, Kenwood made each of them take turns saying Grace before they ate. He felt that the Lord should be thanked for allowing them to fill their stomachs with each passing day. Regardless of how shy Kendall was, when it came his turn to say Grace he had no choice. Sensing he was uncomfortable, his siblings both tried to ease his unwillingness to speak and even told jokes to make him laugh before he had to speak. Sometimes it worked but most of the time, Kendall would turn beet red whenever he had to recite a prayer that was memorized by heart. His face would blush and his cheeks would turn rosy-red. His parents and siblings were used to his face turning all shades of red as he grew into a young man. During his school years it was truly anything but a learning experience. Kendall's teachers, with many parent conferences, realized his unusual situation both with his growth spurt and his inability to speak in front of strangers. Even his peers watched as he tried to participate in class but couldn't. With the teachers constant supervision, Kendall was lucky that he wasn't picked on. In class he was left alone to do his work and on the very few times when he was called upon, seeing him blush from cheek to cheek, kept the teachers from choosing him to answer questions. So Kendall remained a loner with none of the other children choosing to be his friends. Kenrich and Daisy were total opposites from him. With their blond hair and blues eyes resembling both their parents, they were the most popular among their peers. Groups of children would follow them around just to be in their company. Kenrich was a great public speaker and loved to speak in front of large groups. Daisy, too, had no problem getting up in front of an audience. Many Sunday lectures were now the responsibility of the two well-adjusted Peterson children. Both Kenrich and Daisy were spiritually blessed as well, pleasing Kenwood beyond imagination. Kendall, of course, wasn't. Kendall would get butterflies in his stomach and feel like his heart would beat right through his chest whenever he had to talk to more than one person face to face. Usually he kept his head down never making eye contact. And being less than four feet tall made it easier to do that. Add the full white beard at such an early age and his deep brown eyes and you had a creepy combination, keeping most people from wanting to talk to him. Kenwood, his father, resorted to keeping him busy in every other area of the parish instead of up on the pulpit. Upon graduating from high school he refused to get a job. He couldn't deal with the public. He preferred to stay home whenever he could. His parents knew he wouldn't change and refused to make a bigger issue out of it. They truly loved him in spite of all his insecurities. His chores and growing responsibilities to the upkeep of the Church made it easier for his parents to accept the fact that he really couldn't deal with outside employment. Life was anything but peaceful for a preacher's son. Kendall, too, prayed that his shyness around people would change and that he could finally be accepted. As he became a young man, he hoped that his attitude would improve along with his confidence. Knowing that he was destined to be a loner he decided to keep clear of all people other than his immediate family. Kendall would even perform his duties for the church in the evening. As the years continued one to the other, Kendall became more of a hermit, only leaving his house during the night. Parishioners, realizing he was never present, didn't question the preacher or his wife. Rumors circulated that Kendall was now just too shy to be around people. Whenever the Petersons did accept an offer for dinner at a neighbor's home, they now chose to leave Kendall home.

Kenwood, Delia, Kenrich and Daisy were quite a talkative bunch and also very well liked within the town of Hickabee. As it stood now both Kenwood and Delia looked forward to someone else's home cooked meals and a pleasant evening out. No longer did they have to fight with Kendall just to leave the house. An evening away in the company of neighbors was very much desired. Kendall was left alone to go about his business and cherished his alone time. He would finish what needed tending to at the Church and spend the next couple of hours down by the riverbank. The stream that ran from their property led into a larger riverbank, which flowed into the Great White Bay. Yards from their property sat the stream. Kendall would sneak down to the river and lazily lounge by its side for hours on end, always heading back home before sunrise. After his peaceful time alone, he would crawl back into bed making sure not to disturb his sleeping family.

His parents would pretend that they were aware of his desire to spend hours alone down by the river. Kenwood would silently pray for his son each Sunday before service asking the good Lord to help break his middle child out of his shell. And every week his prayers for Kendall would go unanswered. The stunted growth and lack of self-confidence would be a burden for Kendall as well as his entire family for as long as Kendall walked this glorious earth. In order to help deal with his own issues concerning Kendall, Kenwood focused on the needs of his parishioners who for some odd reason always overcame their troubles.

Tonight, however, Kendall rushed through his evening chores to head directly to the riverbank. Pressing issues were troubling him. Daisy, his younger sister, had asked him to go the local square dance, which was a yearly event held in Hickabee. The dance was months away and Daisy gave him ample notice to prepare himself mentally. Kendall knew Daisy was trying to help him to become more social and that she could have any fine gentleman caller take her instead. For that reason alone he was grateful for the love of his sister. But deep down, he knew he could never step foot in the huge barn that held the event. With the hundreds of townspeople that would turn out for the annual festival, Kendall would most certainly go into a panic.

How he would come up with an excuse as to not hurt his sister was something he didn't want to think about right at the moment. Pushing the thought from his mind he lay down near the edge of the river and listened to the water that rushed past him. Kendall knew he couldn't get too comfortable lying there staring at the millions of stars up in the sky. The heavy rains from the day before caused flooding which always left the river higher than normal. The edge of the river overflowed around most of the areas where he usually relaxed. This one spot where he now laid was still unaffected by the rising waters. As he focused on the peace and quiet of his surroundings, he heard a small cry that made him sit up. Not exactly sure if it was a cry of a baby or of an animal, Kendall stood up and looked around where he thought he had heard the noise. Skeptical at first, he stood there and listened when he heard the cry for a second time. The sound was much louder than the first confirming his reasoning that it was indeed that of an infant. Kendall's eyes started to dart around the woods. Suddenly, off in the distance he thought he saw the figure of a person running through the trees. Almost certain it was a human and not an animal, Kendall headed toward the running person, who by now was almost out of sight. Kendall sped up but with such tiny legs found it difficult to catch up to the person who had since vanished into the woods. Kendall felt like he had run for miles when in fact he barely covered much distance.

When he stopped to finally catch his breath, the wails of a crying baby were very nearby.

Forgetting about the person who moments ago stood close to this exact spot, Kendall was certain that the infant was in some sort of trouble. No one should be near this edge of the river especially at this time of night. The rising water had washed away some of the smaller rocks that lined the skirts of the water. If you weren't careful you could slip and fall into the rushing waters. Death would be inevitable. No one ever came down to the riverbank at these late hours. The crying baby was no longer wailing but its voice took on a screaming pitch that startled Kendall. He knew he had to act fast. Making his way carefully to the edge of the river, he spotted what appeared to be a basket leaning too close to the edge of the river. Kendall watched as the rising water moved the basket with the crying baby a couple of inches inward at first. A blue blanket hung over one side of the wooden basket. The water now started to rock the basket from side to side moving it more as it did. Kendall stepped over some fallen tree stumps and closed the distance between him and the terrified baby who now was soaked with the rising waters. Kendall was knee high himself in the water which had spread farther into the woods. He had only seconds before the wooden basket would be taken into the river and swept away.

Kendall grabbed hold of the basket and lifted it up with the little baby now safely in his arms. Kendall had saved the infant's life. If he hadn't been down at the river that evening this poor baby would have drowned. Kendall made his way out of the woods carrying the basket and headed to his home. This time he would have to wake up his parents. Kendall didn't know what to do with the baby who had quieted down now that he had retrieved him. Kenwood and Delia would take over from there. They would find out why and how the tiny infant was left abandoned, leaving Kendall to go back to his obscure life.

The only thing Kendall didn't realize when he rescued the baby boy in the town of Hickabee, was he would now always be remembered as a hero.

◆

As it turned out, the baby boy belonged to a young, unattractive woman by the name of Hanna. Hanna was not well known in the town of Hickabee, simply because she was an unwed woman. Most villagers frowned upon this state and ignored her. As she was a simple woman with rather plain features her image was not helped much and people didn't pay attention to her. The villagers did know of her infant son and were delighted that Kendall had rescued the child. They were, however, skeptical of the explanation that she had given as to why her baby ended up by the riverbank. Hanna claimed she had been walking along the riverbank as she so often had since his birth. Hanna claimed that her son was colic and the rushing water soothed him so he could sleep. That night, she stated that while she was walking, she lost her footing and fell into the river but by the grace of God wound up grabbing onto a very large floating tree branch that eventually got stuck downstream, enabling her to make her way to safety.

She was desperately trying to make it by foot to look for her child upstream along the bank but the rocks were slippery and very dangerous. The next morning her neighbors, upon first seeing her, informed her that her child was safe. Hanna ran to Town's Square where she was reunited with her baby. After Kenwood gave the infant a special blessing for a long life, he and Delia were more than happy to hand over the child to his hysterical mother.

Hanna gave her best performance when she explained the saga of her separation from her child. The townspeople had no other choice but to believe her story. Still many suspicious villagers said they would now keep a careful eye on her and her infant son to make sure she didn't have any unlikely accidents again. She would have to stay in the village and raise her son with no chance of leaving. If she did they would track her down and bring both she and her child back. And, in the unlikely event her child wasn't with her when they found her, then she would be punished in a fashion she was told they would rather not mention. Hanna now knew they didn't truly trust her and would now have no choice but to raise this unwanted burden of hers in a town which hated her. Luckily for her she overheard her neighbors from her bedroom window early the following morning talking about an infant having been saved down by the water's edge. She was furious and how the little nuisance could have been saved baffled her. She was certain after finding the perfect spot that no one was even remotely close by. She had everything planned out so perfectly. With the rising waters it

127

should have worked. The brat should have sailed away to whatever fate awaited him. She didn't care either way. But he didn't. It ruined all her future dreams. The following day she intended on staying in all day. That night she would leave the rotten village of Hickabee in search of a town where she could start anew without the scars of having a child out of wedlock. She had hoped to be accepted in this town where she chose to have her baby, but as it turned out she was wrong. Hanna hoped for a new town where people would at least glance in her direction. To a town where she could meet the right man and this time get married first before bearing his children. Not like the loser who had tricked her into sleeping with him with no intention of marrying her. His quest was to sleep with a virgin and he achieved his goal. When Hanna told him she was expecting he wanted nothing to do with her and made her pregnancy miserable in their town. The father of her child spread malicious rumors about her throughout the town, which ensured that no one bothered with her. At first Hanna tried, to no avail, to miscarry the baby. Realizing she was doomed to carry the baby full term, she had no choice but to move onto Hickabee. Hanna was miserable. Her grand plan had failed. So, upon hearing that her son had survived, she threw on some ragged looking clothing and from her yard smeared some mud on her face and hands as well as her clothes. Afterwards, Hanna ran out from the backyard looking like a frantic, panicked mother. The neighbors took her by the arms and comforted her reassuring her that her baby was safe. Hanna would have to play the role of distraught mother, which she knew she could pull off. As she headed to claim this life-long obligation, she swore revenge on the individual who saved her child and by doing so had ruined her life.

◆

The town was elated when they heard that Kendall had rescued the infant. Kenwood and Delia were so proud of their son and at every opportunity relayed the story in detail to listening ears. Over the next couple of days, people couldn't stop talking about Kendall's bravery in risking his own life to save the infant that would surely have drowned. The mayor, himself, of the town of Hickabee wanted to personally congratulate Kendall. Many other board members of the community council felt the same. Residents from all over the town felt some sort of ceremony should take place honoring Kendall and that he should be given some sort of recognition for his heroism on that dreary night just a few days past. The mayor decided to present Kendall with a plaque and a ribbon along with his own key to the village. Mayor McKeever, along with the board members, decided the sooner the better and set the date for the upcoming weekend. The event would take place Saturday late afternoon right in Town's Square where hundreds of townspeople could gather to hear Kendall tell his own tale of the rescue of the infant. Afterwards, a celebration would take place with food and music from the various street vendors. A festive time for the whole village being the annual square dance was still many weeks away. Hickabee could use a boost to liven the town up and the Mayor felt that having a hero among them would do just that. The only thing left to do was for Mayor McKeever to personally invite Kendall. After that, the only other thing left to do, was to convince Kendall that he needed to be there for the ceremony.

◆

Blushing as he had so often done, Kendall fought to protest the inevitable, "I can't! I won't! Neither of you can convince me to go up on that podium and speak to a crowd of hundreds. No way and that is the end of it."

"You're being ridiculous about this whole thing. Honestly, Kendall, the whole town is eager to congratulate you in person and you don't want them to. Explain to me why. All you have to do is tell the story as it happened. Easy enough. No one is looking for more than that. The Mayor is delighted to present you with an award. An award! Can you imagine?" his mother said sitting next to him in the family room of their small house.

"Really, Mother, it was no big deal. Anyone could have done it," Kendall answered in an increasingly nervous voice.

"No big deal!" His father, who been quiet long enough said, "Do you realize the impact you've had on this town? EVERYONE is amazed at how someone and how should I say it. Someone so... No. Someone of shorter than average height not only saved the infant, but was able to carry the baby from the water without being swept away, as well."

His brother joined in, "Besides, we'll be there to support you. I'll even help you write down your story so all you have to do is read it. Simple as that! You can do it. I know you can. I'm so proud of you. Even my friends want to shake hands with someone who would risk his own life to do what you did."

"Please, for all of us! If you do accept the award, you'll make mother and father so happy. I mean look how they light up when people stop them to congratulate them on having raised a son like you. We really want this for you, Kendall. Please, do this for me," His younger sister pleaded knowing her asking would make him give it some real consideration.

Kendall was defeated. As much as he feared speaking in public, he knew he could never let his family down. The love that they all shared was something he was grateful for even if he chose to be a loner. All he had to do was read what Kenrich would help him write. According to Daisy, the Mayor would then present him with a whole bunch of goodies. Maybe this would help him to get used to people once and for all. After all, he truly was a hero. Kendall shook his head in agreement and finally answered yes. Hearing his answer made his overly delighted family jump up from their seats and run up to hug him for his bravery in accepting his award. They all knew this would be very difficult for him to accomplish. Kendall felt all their arms around his tiny body and blushed in a good way this time. After all, maybe it wouldn't be so bad, Kendall thought, but little did he know how bad it really would become.

◆

Hanna had to go and see this individual who had saved her son who tormented her so. Many of her neighbors had spoken so highly of this little man who was a hermit. Hanna had never seen him for herself. Eager to catch a glimpse of the tiny person who saved her bastard of a son and destroyed her life in the process, she watched for him to leave his house to go to his cleaning job at the church. Her nosy next-door neighbors filled her in on all of Kendall's activities. With just two days to go before the ceremony to honor this small man, Hanna had to see him ahead of time. Mayor McKeever wanted Hanna to present Kendall with the plaque while holding her repulsive child. Hanna pretended she was honored to be chosen to do so. Upon hearing that an award was to be given, she knew it would be her luck to have to present it. Nothing was going her way and probably never would. As her eyes glanced in the direction of the disgusting little being that spoiled her plans, she gasped at how someone so little could have sabotaged, though innocently, all her plans. Hanna stood there staring into space after Kendall had left and entered the church. Hanna vowed to find out everything there was to know about this tiny man. With the information she acquired, she would find a way to destroy him as he did her. Hanna knew she would find some way to humiliate this man the day of the ceremony. What Hanna didn't realize was just how easy it would be.

◆

Saturday morning came sooner than Kendall had hoped. He had hardly slept a wink that night with all the tossing and turning he did. Images of himself up on the podium reading his well-written speech, prepared by Kenrich, had him breaking out in a cold sweat. Kendall was in a near panic as he rose to the aroma of breakfast coming from the kitchen. Delia would treat all her children to their favorite breakfast once a year on their birthdays. Today was a happy occasion for Kendall and he deserved special treatment, which he wasn't really used to. His mother cooked all his favorites, which included pancakes, sausage, and bacon, along with scrambled eggs and toast that she had placed on his plate. Kendall was too upset to eat. Sensing his nervousness, Delia tried to lighten the moment with some of his favorite bedtime stories from when he was a child. Nothing seemed to break him out of his state of panic. Kendall's face was beet red as he sat at the kitchen table. Kendall stayed there for the remainder of the morning and into the afternoon without moving or saying a word. He wished that he could vanish into thin air. When the time to leave finally arrived, Kendall knew he had no choice but to get on with the celebration that he wasn't exactly ready for. Feeling his pain, the entire Peterson family prayed for Kendall to accept his award with his head held high. Delia prayed the hardest for her second son. She prayed he would be okay and make it through the ceremony. But deep down in her heart, her mother's intuition told her to be prepared. To be very prepared for just about anything to happen.

◆

As they first approached the center of Town Square, Kenrich and Daisy stood on each side of Kendall reassuring him that he would be fine and everything would be okay. Hundreds of villagers were already gathered. Kenwood and Delia made their way first into the square. Mayor McKeever had some of the townsmen set up a stage five feet off the ground. On the stage was a podium with three rows of chairs off to one side. The chairs were reserved for Kendall's family, Hanna, and for the Chamber members of the town of Hickabee. As Kendall entered the square, he suddenly stopped walking, which necessitated Kenrich and Daisy dragging him along. Kendall froze when he first saw the very large audience. Kenwood walked back to them and whispered into his son's ear that he was truly a hero and that he was so proud of him. Kendall, shocked from what he heard his father tell him, proceeded to walk on his own. His father had never said anything like that to him before. Kenrich and Daisy, surprised to see the sudden change, let go of his arms. Kendall couldn't believe his father whispered those five simple words that meant the world to him. Kendall could do it and would do it. After all, his father was so proud of him. Kendall picked up his pace and led the rest of the family to the stage while the crowd of hundreds cheered and applauded as he walked by. The noise was deafening to Kendall so he covered his ears as he walked up to the stage. Mayor McKeever greeted him first while the crowd continued cheering. Kenwood, Delia, Kenrich and Daisy all took their seats next to Hanna and the rescued baby boy. Mayor McKeever waited for the audience to calm down. Once the crowd had settled, the Mayor stepped up to the podium and began the ceremony. Kendall felt his bravery from moments ago slipping fast. All those eyes were on Kendall as the Mayor continued his praise for him. Kendall wanted nothing more than to deliver his speech, receive his award and be far, far away from all those people who now stood staring at him. The attention was making him very uncomfortable. The Mayor finished his introduction and it was time for Kendall to make his long dreaded speech that he had rehearsed over and over in his head. The crowd began to clap again. Louder than when he first walked into the square. Kendall covered his ears from the loud applause. He should have enjoyed the applause because in just minutes the laughter that soon would follow would all but kill him.

◆

Kendall took three steps up to the podium and realized he couldn't see over the top.

The podium was close to five feet tall and made of oak. He wasn't nearly tall enough to see over it. Standing behind the podium, no one in the crowd could see him. The podium blocked his view. Mayor McKeever, taking Kendall's tiny height into consideration when he had the stage set, had made sure five empty milk crates were placed to the left side of the podium. He had planned to place them in front of the podium just as Kendall stepped up to it. Baffled at why they had disappeared, the Mayor looked from side to side for the missing crates. The crowd started to shout out that they still couldn't see him. Others were yelling for someone to pick him up so they could get a view of him. The whole scene was starting to get ugly. Mayor McKeever was frantic to find something to elevate poor Kendall, who started to blush from cheek to cheek and was now losing all his confidence. Kenwood and Delia stood up to find anything to make their son look taller while the crowd continued to yell because they couldn't see him. Kenrich, his brother, spotted what looked like two hidden milk crates, jumped off the stage, grabbed the crates and ran around the stairs and up onto the stage again. Mayor McKeever, needing to react quickly, took the crates and placed them in front of the podium. Kenwood took hold of Kendall and helped him get up onto the two crates. Kendall stood atop the crates and still wasn't visible to the audience in the back. His head of white hair was the only part of him that was clearly seen. Everyone in the back of the crowd started to laugh at the scene that started to unfold. It was starting to look like a circus act rather than an award ceremony. Hanna smiled as she watched the event turn out exactly as she had planned. She stood up with her unwanted baby in her arms. Hanna had arrived at the Center of Town Square earlier than everyone else. She knew no one would pay any attention to her, as long as she carried her infant with her, and proceeded with her master plan. She placed her son whom she despised down on the stage and quickly grabbed the milk crates. One by one she hid them. Realizing the excitement would be overwhelming for everyone gathered, Hanna hoped no one would miss the crates needed to lift this tiny pitiful creature off the ground.

Hanna was right. She did, however, leave two partially hidden crates with the intention of someone seeing them and that worked too. Hanna surmised two crates wouldn't be high enough for the creepy little misfit and this proved true as well. She also knew it would look very funny from afar and that the audience would find it amusing to witness. Now, in a state of confusion, the Mayor and the Peterson's were grasping for anything to calm the now roaring laughter from the crowd. Sensing this was her perfect opportunity and knowing it was now or never, Hanna gave her best performance to date. Looking over at a now sweating, blushing, cowering Kendall, Hanna joined in with the madness, "Oh my! Oh my! What do we have here? How could such a big or should I say little for that matter BRAVE man like Kendall look so scared?"

The crowd heard her call Kendall little and started to laugh even louder pointing at him as they did.

Hanna, knowing she was now the crowd pleaser, continued, "This is what saved my baby! We look to present this tiny person with an award for being a hero.

What I see standing in front of me is nothing but a very small shy man. Yes, that's it! This man is nothing but YOURSHYNESS! Yourshyness! Yourshyness! Yourshyness!" Hanna kept repeating that one word over and over again and, what she had wished would happen, did. The villagers who were gathered in the front rows started to chant out the word Hanna kept saying. Yourshyness could be heard among the whole crowd now. People were holding their bellies from the laughter that overcame them. Others were pointed and yelling for Kendall to say something. The whole scene was out of control. Mayor McKeever and other members of the board knew that this could turn into a riot if things weren't brought under control fast.

Kenwood, Delia, Kenrich, and Daisy looked on in disbelief. Most of these townspeople had filled their Church every Sunday. They called themselves Christians and followed the good word of the Lord. Kenwood wanted nothing more than to know just which Lord they followed. Certainly not the one he held most High. After taking Kendall away from this hostility, Kenwood would later pray to redeem all these lost souls. First he would comfort his now and always to remain introverted son. Kenwood rushed to Kendall's side, but it was too late. Kendall had run with all his might off the stage and into the laughing crowd who had parted to let him through. As a humiliated Kendall ran he knew he would never be able to stay in the town of Hickabee. Kendall didn't want to be around people ever again. Kendall knew what he must do. He would leave the town and never return. He didn't care where he went. He just couldn't be around people anymore, including his family whom he knew, he would miss for all of eternity. Kendall ran right through the crowd and out of sight. Hanna rocked her burdened baby and watched the mini-man run off. She had stopped chanting the name that would stick with Kendall forever. Hanna had repaid Kendall with her promise for revenge and won. She, too, disappeared into the crowd knowing she could never truly be free from this town, but just hearing the crowd still scream out Yourshyness made it all the more worthwhile.

◆

Kendall ran straight home. He threw together some clothes and shoved them in a knapsack. He would hide down at the riverbank and wait until the stroke of midnight.

His family would be heartbroken about his disappearance at first but knew with their strength in the good Lord that they, too, would overcome this hardship and move on. Kendall left the small house he knew he would never call home again. He waited down at what used to be his favorite spot near the river's edge. The spot where this whole nightmare began. He waited and waited. Kendall, judging by the position of the moon overhead, knew it was midnight. He stood up, grabbed his knapsack and left for the only other place he knew. Kendall headed directly to the Black Forest.

12

"What da we do? How we gonna get to em?" Cranky said in a voice nearing panic.

Emdee who always took control of any situation tired to calm the five of them down,

"Let me sink, I mean think. Yeah, let me think. There's got to be a way to get through that tunnel of dust. There just has to be!"

Toodum, who was smarter than he was given credit for, ran downstairs and returned in a short time carrying what looked like rope. Before Toodum handed it to Cranky, he had made a lasso out of the rope. Cranky took the rope from Toodum and knew just what he wanted them to do. Without speaking, Toodum made the remaining five know exactly what he intended for them to do to rescue Yourshyness from the other side of the room. Using the rope as a lasso they could throw it over Yourshyness and pull him through the mini-tornado that swirled around their bedroom.

With force Emdee, Cranky and Merry together tossed the rope through the wind and toward Yourshyness. They kept missing their target. Time after time they continued to throw the lasso just missing Yourshyness each time. Dozzey, Toodum and Hachew stood near by watching their futile attempts. Cranky gave it his best effort with the other two and tossed the lasso this time landing directly around Yourshyness. The three of them pulled the lasso tighter around Yourshyness and pulled with all their might. Slowly, they were making progress when all of a sudden the windstorm stopped and Emdee, Cranky, and Merry fell to the ground. The dust that was in a whirlwind dropped to the floor. Yourshyness, who had since come out of his trance, had safely been pulled to the landing at the top of the stairs joining the others. With a look of panic still in his eyes, he needed to get far away from the bedroom. Emdee had had enough and was instructing the other six to just go back downstairs. Six of them were at the first step leading down. Hachew who was just as anxious to get far away from their bedroom had the urge to sneeze. Cranky, who had experienced some of Hachew's sneezes, knew what was coming. Hachew had a tendency to sneeze with such force that he could blow anyone clear across a room depending on how long he tried to hold it in. Hachew tried to concentrate on escaping the wrath of the others and by doing so held in his sneeze. He held back his head and with no luck, released one of his biggest sneezes yet. One gigantic Hachoo. Emdee, Cranky, Dozzey, Merry, Yourshyness and Toodum were all blown away and tumbled down the stairs. None of them were hurt. Hachew, from the impact of his own sneeze, was thrown across the bedroom. He sailed through the air and landed on the floor sliding straight in front of his own bed. Sensing the sheer terror the other five had experienced, he tried to move but found himself stuck. An evil spell, he was convinced, held him in place. Dreading the inevitable and fearing the worst, he too, paid a visit to a much painful memory from so long ago.

Eugenist Wibbles

A little man with whose health there is nothing doctors can do, So he shall be given the name of HACHEW.......

-Helga

13

In a quaint and peaceful village, a not so quiet elfish baby was delivered. Eugenist Wibbles was his given name. His tiny size startled his parents when the midwife handed him over to Eugenist's momma. Schneider and Penelope Wibbles had tried unsuccessfully for many years to conceive the small infant son they now held. Approaching mid-life Penelope's fertility decreased making it all the more difficult for her to become pregnant. According to the town doctor, the chances were slim for the couple who wanted nothing more than to start a family. Never giving up, together they beat the odds and their little bundle of joy was born. Regardless of his stunted frame, Schneider and Penelope adored their first child. Until, early on when they became concerned about his constant sneezing. Eugenist, such a tiny infant, sneezed so often and with such great force that his poppa, Schneider, found this amusing at first. How an itsy bitsy baby boy could sneeze so loudly and with a small wind from his nostrils blow his hair back. Penelope had never in her lifetime seen anything quite like it.

Alarmed she brought Eugenist, who was now three months old, to the town doctor.

Duggandorf was a medium-sized town. The population neared one thousand residents within the village. Schneider and Penelope lived above the cookie factory that they owned. Schneider had possession of a family recipe passed down to him for oatmeal cookies for which the townspeople could never get enough. It was a secret family recipe started by Schneider's grandfather. A recipe that he could now pass down to his son, Eugenist. The shop was right in the middle of Duggandorf. Two pubs, a general store, a clothier, and a bank flanked the cookie store on both sides. The Wibbles lived in a two-bedroom apartment above the shops in the building they owned. Upon arriving in Duggandorf many years prior from a town less fortunate, the Wibbles found the building for rent, and with money inherited from Schneider's deceased parents, purchased the store. Schneider and Penelope put in many long hours turning the shop into a factory for baking cookies.

They installed three large ovens capable of making dozens of cookies in each batch.

Schneider, himself, handmade the long counter along the front of the store for customers who came in to place their orders. Penelope ran the front end of the business, taking orders and handling the books, while Schneider did all the baking of the oatmeal cookies according to the secret family recipe. Before sunrise, both Schneider and Penelope would rise, go downstairs, and start their day in the factory. They usually worked straight through the day with quitting time at five o'clock. Around the holidays they worked into the wee hours of the evening. Most nights they were too exhausted from a hard day at the factory and went to bed early without any supper. This lifestyle could also have been a factor in their inability to start a family. But, all in all, they both truly loved their work.

Now as Penelope listened to Doctor Shaw ease her concerns over Eugenist's constant fits of sneezing, telling her other than his small size, he was a healthy normal boy. She knew it was more than allergies that Eugenist had though he was still too young to be tested. Penelope sensed this was only the beginning of a problem that would linger on for many years to come.

◆

Eugenist continued sneezing right into his toddler years. When he turned four, two major events took place in the Wibbles family household. First, Doctor Shaw tested little Eugenist for allergies. He was still much shorter than normal with no signs of any real growth spurts. As it turned out, Eugenist was most allergic to ragweed causing him a severe case of hay fever. The ragweed pollen was airborne making it easier to reach Eugenist's nostrils. One of the symptoms most acute for Eugenist was his sneezing fits. Knowing about his condition made Eugenist's parents more calm whenever he would start his sneezing spells that could last for minutes at a time. The sneezing wasn't all that bad; it was the force from the sneeze that still upset them. No longer amusing to Schneider, on more than one occasion he would have to place a finger under his young son's nostrils hoping to stop his sneezing. As soon as tiny Schneider rolled his head back a sneeze was sure to follow. As a telltale sign that a sneeze or many were about to take place, Schneider would drop everything and run to place a finger under his nose. It was a never-ending battle that both he and his wife Penelope were not willing to give up. Whoever spotted Eugenist with his head tilting back would call out to the other and whoever was closest would assume the responsibility. When given the correct amount of notice, the results proved in their favor and they were able to stifle the sneezes. When they came up short the results were anything but good. Many pieces of fine china, glassware and other valuable items were lost because of the magnitude of his sneezes. Now accustomed to the forceful breezes that could muster up and come out of such a tiny individual, Eugenist's parents hid anything that could be blown away. Furniture that couldn't be hidden and was too fragile they bolted to the floors. But overall, regardless of his few misfortunes, they loved him quite dearly.

The second event that pleased Schneider, Penelope and even little Eugenist, was the birth of his baby sister, Elphaba. Proving once again that the statistics of a second pregnancy were not absolute, Penelope gave birth to a healthy little girl and that completed their dreams of having a perfect family. Perfect in every sense of the word, for the time being anyway.

◆

Running a successful cookie business, watching your two children grow into young adults, was everything that Penelope could have wanted. From the very beginning, Eugenist worshipped his baby sister and watched over her like a hawk. No one could say a bad word about her. Whether she cried all night, refused to eat her baby food, or wouldn't take a bath, Eugenist always came to her rescue before any punishments could be implemented. While their parents were working downstairs, Eugenist, from an early age, was entrusted to take care of his sister. This daily task, which would have been a burden for most, delighted him. As Elphaba grew, her love for her brother was growing and becoming enormous. The two of them spent their childhood years side by side playing for hours on end.

Many villagers envied the love these siblings shared with one another after witnessing them together. Most brothers and sisters were at each other's throats, which was never the case with Eugenist and Elphaba. Even throughout their school years together, the two were inseparable. Elphaba was the only person able to truly accept Eugenist for who he was including his faults. Elphaba even tolerated his fits of sneezing, which had long since grown annoying to his parents. Elphaba would slide across any floor to the other side of a room to try to help prevent an oncoming sneeze. When she couldn't catch the sneeze in time she would join in the fun and fake the hachoo along with her brother. The two of them would laugh so hard afterwards that Eugenist would again suffer an attack. Whether it really was hay fever didn't matter anymore since anything could trigger an episode. The remaining Wibbles learned to adjust and knew that they would always have to live with Eugenist and his sneezing. Then other elements came into play that made it more difficult for Eugenist. While they were young, Elphaba grew at a rate that surpassed her tiny older brother, but she always made it seem like it was no big deal. Elphaba, at five feet six inches tall, had brown hair and green eyes that she inherited from both her parents. Her poppa was six feet tall and her momma was five inches shorter. Eugenist, on the other hand, had hair that had gone prematurely gray. Toward his late teens he had grown a full white beard that matched the top of his head. His growth had stopped years prior to his hair turning white. At no more than four feet tall, with stunted arms and legs, his appearance was eerie until you really got to know him. Elphaba, loving him so deeply, was never put off by his appearance. Throughout their school years when other children would glance and even tease Eugenist, it was now Elphaba who came to his defense. His fits of sneezing disrupted the class and caused many outbursts of laughter among their peers. The teachers had been well informed of his condition and when Eugenist tilted his head back, they made a point to stay far far away.

Sometimes the class would join in and together as one they would yell out hachoo just as Eugenist had another fit of sneezing. This bothered her brother immensely and Elphaba would put a stop to it whenever she caught them doing it. Her older brother was her world and she would not allow anyone to disrupt it. It was a world only the two of them could appreciate. So as the two of them grew into the fine adults they were, life seemed once again perfect for the Wibbles, too perfect. So perfect until the day when Eugenist was asked to help take over the family business.

◆

"Poppa, what do you mean I have to do it all? What if I can't bake them as well as you?

People from Duggandorf and from towns miles away come for your family recipe of oatmeal cookies. I'm not so sure about this," Eugenist who was standing along side his father mixing the cookie dough said. In his usual calm voice and with the reassurance that Eugenist had become so familiar with Poppa answered, "Give yourself more credit than that my son. You CAN run the business and you WILL make the cookies to perfection. You've been helping me for how long now? Four years if my memory serves me correct. Time for your momma and me to retire and let you and your sister take over the business. Your momma has been wanting to travel for years now. We're getting on in age and with you two still in your twenties we know you are both very capable and able to handle all areas of the store like your momma and I have done for all these years. When you and your sister start your own families then you can pass along the tradition that has been a secret recipe for generations to them. Now stop all this worrying and bring me over the dough you've been mixing for the last twenty minutes."

"I guess you're right, Poppa. You and Momma deserve to travel and enjoy retirement.

It was very selfish of me to deny you that privilege. I owe you a lot and I am grateful for the opportunities you have given me. Here you go, Poppa," Eugenist finished as he placed the large mixing bowl up on the counter. The batch of oatmeal cookies was ready to be put onto the cookies sheets for baking in the large ovens that were lined up across the back wall of the store. His poppa smiled as he took the bowl and started to spread the dough into tiny circles on the cookies pans. Schneider was proud of how he had raised his two children and wanted nothing more for them than to succeed in life.

The only thing he didn't realize was that one of them would almost lose their life.

◆

For the next few months Eugenist and Elphaba ran the cookie factory. Business was booming and together they were a successful team. The money was plentiful. They gave any excess money to their parents so that Schneider and Penelope could continue to enjoy the luxury of traveling. Customers came to the store constantly. Elphaba would take orders, write up receipts and figure out exactly how many batches her brother would have to make. The oatmeal cookies flew off the shelves faster than she could stock them. Children would run into the shop with change from their parents and buy some cookies to eat fresh from the oven. Rack upon rack of daily cookies were bought before the close of their day. So as it was, one day led to the next and weeks went into months never slowing down enough for Eugenist and Elphaba to catch their breath. As long as they were in each other's company, they were satisfied with their lives and their daily routine. They would live their lives one day at a time. Until the one day when the old woman entered the store and changed their lives forever.

◆

Once a week Elphaba would run over to the general store to buy some ingredients for the recipe. These ingredients were not a secret part of the family tradition. However, they were still needed to make the oatmeal cookies. Many villagers would ask the owner of the general store what the Wibbles actually purchased in order to try to duplicate the recipe, but no one in the village ever came close. After a while it became clear that the Wibbles' oatmeal cookies were indeed the best cookies not only in the town of Duggandorf, but in most of the nearby towns as well. Usually Wednesday was errand day for Elphaba. She would leave around ten in the morning and would be back before noon and the busy lunch crowd that followed. This particular Wednesday she left on schedule, leaving Eugenist to run the store by himself. Just as she left, an old woman walked in. Elphaba and the elderly woman missed each other by a matter of seconds. The two of them would have bumped into one another if Elphaba were delayed for even a fraction of a minute. Eugenist watched the old woman, who seemed to be carrying something in a brown paper bag, push open the door and slowly enter the store. The woman looked to be close to eighty with her gray hair pulled tightly in a bun up on her head. Her face and hands were very wrinkled and as she got closer, he could see her dull blue eyes seemed lifeless. She was maybe a foot taller than he making her no taller than five feet. He had seen her come in over the years but never really knew who she was. She definitely was not one of their regular customers but rather a customer who had stopped in and bought on occasion. Penelope, his momma, would sometimes make a comment when she left the store about how sorry she felt for this woman. Eugenist had overheard her tell his poppa more than once how life was so cruel to some people. From putting together bits and pieces of the last conversation his parents had about this old woman, Eugenist gathered it had to do with her never having married. Also, something else about her sister or sisters that did wed.

Either way he knew she missed out on her opportunity to get married. Now, as she approached the counter, Eugenist wiped his hands on his apron and in his usual cheery voice greeted her, "Good morning ma'am. How can I help you? Would you like to place an order or purchase some oatmeal cookies right off the shelve?"

The old woman set the brown paper bag down on the counter and smiled. With the few teeth that she had remaining she introduced herself, "My name's Helga. I've been coming to this store since before you two were even born. Usually three to four times a year. I know your name is Eugenist and your pretty sister is Elphaba. I know all about you. I'm here because I have something for you."

Eugenist stared at this old woman who acted as though she had known him. He was becoming more confused by the second by this woman. He watched as she reached inside the brown paper bag and pulled out a jar with some type of human skull and crossbones that criss-crossed right below it. A word in some language he had never seen before was written underneath the skull. He had never seen a bottle of that type with the skull of a human inside. Eugenist questioned this frail older woman who stared at him with the saddest eyes he had ever seen.

"What's the bottle for? I mean what's in it? And what is that strange word written on the bottle," he asked.

"For a young man, you certainly ask a lot of questions. First, inside the jar are some diced apples from my very own apple tree. Secondly, they're for you. And the writing is Latin for precious," Helga answered. She continued, "I want you to do me a favor. I have been eating these oatmeal cookies for years and could never quite put my finger on what they needed. Then it hit me. Some of my precious apples mixed in the dough would provide a truly unique taste. I took the liberty of already cutting them up into some really tiny pieces and all you have to do is stir them into the batter. I want you to use the dough with my apples in a couple of your next batches. See what the other townsfolk think. After all, it can't do you any harm."

"How do I know these precious apples are any good? What if my customers don't like them? I mean, who are you? Really. You walk into our store and ask me to try a new ingredient as if it were nothing. These oatmeal cookies don't need anything else. They're fine just the way they are!" Eugenist snapped, noticing that the old woman was staring into his eyes. The next part of her plan was crucial. All of a sudden her gaze changed and she appeared to look ill. Her features suddenly turned pale. Feeling bad for having just snapped, Eugenist offered to get her a glass of water from the back and she kindly accepted. Helga was leaning on the counter like she was about to faint. Eugenist hurried by turning around and going to get her something to drink. Knowing he would be back shortly, Helga knew she would have to act fast and took the potion from the inside pocket of her long black overcoat. She took the small vial, opened the top, and poured a little white powder into her small frail hand.

Eugenist held a glass of water as he came back and handed it to her over the counter. Helga leaned back off the counter and with her other hand she took the water and sipped it. Pretending she was now shaky,

Helga dropped the glass onto the counter and watched it spill over. Eugenist with his quick reflexes scooped up the glass and turned around to grab a towel from the nearby sink. As he glanced away for a brief second, Helga lifted the dust she held in her other hand and with a soft blow, she blew the powder in his direction. In a puff of smoke the white powder disappeared into the air and straight into the path of Eugenist. Eugenist wiped up the water spill and took a deep breath. He wanted to know what was going on with this old woman and her strange ideas about him using her precious apples for the family recipe. She still hadn't answered him. He wanted answers and he wanted them now. As he was about to question her again, he was instantly overcome by a feeling he had never experienced before. Eugenist started to feel a funny or rather odd sensation flow through his body. His mind went blank as he took the jar of diced apples off the counter and opened the lid to pour some out and into one of the large mixing bowls to his right that were filled with dough. Now staring again into his eyes, Helga watched him continue to take the rest using a spatula to scrape the remainder of the tiny pieces of apples into the bowl. He started to mix the diced apples in with the batter. After a few minutes of mixing, he placed the bowl on a tray to bring back to his working area to later spread out onto cookie sheets.

Eugenist didn't know what or why he was doing what he was doing. He did know he was being hypnotized. He was in some type of trance and couldn't break loose from it.

Helga kept her eyes fixed on his and he knew he was in some type of spell. He longed to be free of her grasp. Then, as if on cue and what he had so often done in the past for all of his life, Eugenist tilted his head back. He felt his nostrils start to fill up and he needed to release the sensation he now felt. Eugenist was going to sneeze. Helga, who had heard of his allergies and sneezing fits from many of the other villagers, leaned over the counter and put one of her tiny wiry fingers up against his nose to stop the sneeze. She had once watched his mother, while she was in the store, do that many years ago and it seemed to work. Helga had nothing to lose but try. She held her finger up against his nostril and the urge disappeared. Eugenist didn't sneeze, but he seemed to come out of her spell too soon. As she looked at him, he had a puzzled expression on his face confirming to Helga that he wouldn't remember any of their prior conversation. The powder would take care of his memory loss too. Acting as if nothing out of the ordinary had occurred, Helga took some oatmeal cookies off a shelf and paid for them. Eugenist put the money in the register, bagged her cookies and said goodbye.

Eugenist thanked the old woman for her purchase forgetting all about the apples. He then turned away from her and with both hands grabbed the large mixing bowl filled with Helga's diced apples off the counter. Delighted, Helga continued to watch as he carried the tray back to his working area. As he carried the bowl to the back, Eugenist couldn't fight what happened next. This time no one would stop his sneezing and for the next twenty minutes, Eugenist did just that. Helga, in the mean time said her own goodbye, took the jar with the lid off the counter and placed it back inside the brown paper bag. Eugenist hadn't even noticed the bottle again. Helga had succeeded. Knowing Elphaba would be returning shortly, and not wanting to be seen, Helga fled the store. Later on in the comfort of her cottage, she would rearrange the letters from the word that she made to form precious. By using most of them and also by turning some in other directions she was able to come up with that word to start her plan and help convince Eugenist. The jar was something most villagers had never come across. She searched high and low for the bottle and found it from an old witch doctor from three towns away. Inside the jar was all the elements needed to seal the fate of her one desire. Helga glanced again at the jar.

The bottle was stunning with the skull and two criss-crossed crossbones. What made the jar complete was the lettering that confused poor Eugenist. Precious wasn't really the word in Latin. Helga would later set the original letters back in place to show the one word that would destroy them all. The bad and deadly word that was known as POISON.

◆

Two hours later, Helga sat in her favorite chair by the fireplace. She had her legs up on the ottoman. With a fire blazing in the hearth, Helga sipped the tea she had just poured herself. If all went according to her plan, the next seventy-two hours would be very interesting. The poison that she had searched high and low for would take that long to enter someone's blood stream. That quack of a doctor she had met in the other town sold her the poison. After visiting the seedy areas, continually asking around for something deadly, paying the right person, Helga was given the much-needed connection. For a price, she was given directions to the doctor's house. The doctor had what she wanted and he sold it to her for a hefty price. A price he said would get her any results she needed. He claimed to be a witch doctor that practiced voodoo and all other weird types of magic she had never heard of. To prove the potent effects of the poison, the quack took a chicken out from his coop in his backyard. He poured the liquid into a bowl and let the chicken drink it. As the chicken was relatively small and drank the poison directly, within moments it's eyes began to bulge from their sockets. The creature started to spin in circles as Helga watched. Around and around it went and within a minute dropped to the ground. The chicken was dead. Satisfied, Helga gave most of her life savings and left to put her plan into action.

As Helga continued to drink her tea and eat her biscuits, she thought about her revenge for a town that she despised. Helga hated the town of Duggandorf for as long as she cared to remember. Being the eldest daughter, and least attractive of her seven other sisters, Helga was the only one in the family of all girls not to marry. One by one her beautiful sisters were courted by fine young gentleman within the village. As each sister became old enough to wed, Helga watched as they were each married off and left the dreaded town of Duggandorf for towns more beautiful and filled with opportunity. Helga's parents knew that their eldest daughter was homely and tried to match her with suitable single gentleman within the village. When the gentleman, none whom were very attractive themselves, took one look at Helga they usually suffered through the first date and were never heard from again.

Helga continued to stand in as the sole bridesmaid for each of her younger sisters as they married. Church weddings were small and only one bridesmaid would serve as an attendant to the lucky bride. A maid of honor wasn't heard of until many years later. Her sisters, each pitying her in one way or another, felt it an obligation to have her as their bridesmaid. Knowing she would never marry, her sisters wanted her to get as close as she could to being a bride. At several of the wedding receptions, Helga had overheard some of the guests whisper as she passed an expression that would torment her for years. 'Always a bridesmaid and never a bride' rang true to Helga and hurt just the same. Even as she walked the streets of Duggandorf, villagers would say the expression of the bridesmaid not caring if she heard them or not. Over the years it remained the same. Each of her seven sisters married, moved far away, and left her to care for their aging parents.

Eventually her parents had passed away and Helga had lost all contact with her sisters. Each of them had moved on with families of their own. None of them wanted to be reminded of the ugliest sister of them all. Helga's sisters were too preoccupied with their looks and being beautiful was all that mattered. After all, Helga was the town spinster and that alone was an embarrassment to the seven girls. Leaving Helga alone for most of her adult life had done nothing other than left her wanting to leave the town she most hated. All the villagers had known of her past and that being around them served as a constant reminder of her loneliness. The ugly old maid, who now, because of envy and built up anger, hated them all and only wanted revenge for all the injustice she felt she had suffered. So after coming up with her ingenious plan and mixing the poison in with the diced apples from her tree, Helga smiled when she thought about how easy only hours ago, it was to persuade Eugenist into helping. Helga had studied her own witchcraft from a book of shadows she had come across in an old attic of a house she had cleaned when she worked as a maid during her early years. The old woman, who owned the house, claimed that her ancestors were indeed witches from long ago. Most villagers wrote her off as the town crazywoman and paid her no mind. As the woman aged and became more and more senile Helga, who still cleaned her house, saw her opportunity and snuck the book out to keep as her very own. The crazywoman, too, passed away never realizing her book was missing. Helga, over the years, cherished every chance she had to read the different spells. She even practiced some on the animals who came across her property. Using certain ingredients and mixing her own potions, she concocted her very own special spells. It worked on the animals by just staring into their eyes. She would blow a special powder, usually white, into their faces, and then with only a stare she could control their minds. If she mixed a certain moss from the sacred oak tree into her potion, most of the time the animal wouldn't remember anything it had done while under her spell. Helga had perfected her skills and knew the time was right to destroy the town she most hated. The quack doctor sold her enough poison that if used correctly could kill many, many people. That was exactly what Helga wanted to do. As she was now too old to leave the town of Duggandorf, then just maybe she would make the people of the town do just that. Only their way of leaving was to die, a death that wouldn't be tied into her wrong-doing. Helga knew almost everyone in town bought the famous Wibbles oatmeal cookies. Townspeople from afar came to purchase them too. The following week was the Harvest festival. Everyone brought the Wibbles cookies for that. What better way to rid these hated people than other to mix the poison into the batter of the cookies. A sure way to kill many. Helga knew the elder Wibbles had since traveled a lot leaving the store to their children. She also observed the shop during the past few weeks to see just when her opportunity would arise. The sister, Elphaba, would run an errand every Wednesday to the general store to stock up on certain ingredients. Thursdays and Fridays were craziest at the Wibbles' store. Customers would stock up on the oatmeal cookies for the weekend which would be more so this weekend as the festival was only a week away. Helga knew of Eugenist, the young man who sneezed a lot. She would make certain to point out that one fact when the people of Duggandorf started to die one after another. Helga would blame it on Eugenist and his germs, the germs that finally affected the villagers of Duggandorf. Year after year Eugenist's sneezing spread germs into the mix that eventually caught up to the townspeople. The townspeople that would most certainly die from his germs. Helga knew her plan would work and as she finished her tea and biscuits, she smiled thinking that in just a few short days the population of Duggandorf would decrease dramatically, so drastically that she couldn't wait to savor her revenge.

◆

"Easy! Just how many of those cookies are you going to eat? I've made four batches and by the way, if you keep eating them there won't be any left. You don't see me eating the cookies. I have self-control. Something you lack," Eugenist teased his younger sister.

"Oh, calm down! There are plenty left. Just something about these cookies that's different. A different taste. Did you do anything different to this batch? Did you add a little something special and not tell me? Come on, you can tell me. I won't tell poppa that you are trying to change the secret family recipe," Elphaba said as she poked her older brother in the side.

Eugenist watched Elphaba continue to eat one cookie after another. He took both her hands and held them up as he denied her acquisition, "No, I did NOT do anything different while you were gone. Poppa WOULD kill me if I messed around with the recipe and you know it. Now, quit eating them and start filling the rest of those orders that are on the counter. With the annual Harvest feast next week, we should sell out faster than we have in the past. Almost two thirds of the town will buy our cookies in the next day or two for the festival and most buy one or two cookies to eat while they wait for them in the store. Now stop all this fussing and let's get busy."

♦

As predicated, on those two following days the village of Duggandorf and most of its residents did indeed stock up on the famous Wibbles oatmeal cookies for the harvest festival. As Eugenist insisted was the case, most ate one or two cookies as they waited on the very long line for their order. Business was better than ever and poppa and momma who would be home in time for the festival would be very proud. Elphaba over the last day or so didn't look so good. Her face had gone ashen and her eyes were glazing over in a way that Eugenist had never seen before. That night after dinner, when he questioned her on how she felt, she told him that she didn't feel very well but attributed it to the amount of cookies she had eaten in the last two days. Eugenist felt her forehead and she was on fire. He put her to bed and said if she wasn't better by morning, he would take her to see Doctor Shaw. Even if he had to close the store for the morning rush he would. Elphaba was his world. Now, as he watched his younger sister start to shake, he covered her with layers of blankets. Sweat was breaking out on her face and forehead.

Eugenist was very concerned for her well-being and knew that he wouldn't sleep a wink that evening. He would stay by her bedside for the entire night. Eugenist couldn't imagine how the cookies from his last batch could make her that ill. But, what Eugenist didn't know, was just how many oatmeal cookies Elphaba had hid on the side and eaten on the sly. And what Elphaba didn't realize was just how much of Helga's poison that she consumed.

◆

The following morning Eugenist rushed Elphaba over to Doctor Shaw's office.

Her fever still hadn't broken and she looked even worse. Eugenist lifted her up in his arms and carried her the three short blocks to the doctor. When Eugenist was within a few feet of the entrance, he was confronted by Nurse Jeanita who told him that Doctor Shaw was at town hall. She informed him that a temporary doctor's ward had been set up to accommodate the large volume of very sick patients who had been coming in.

Nurse Jeanita took one look at Elphaba and knew she was in trouble. There was no way she could help her. Doctor Shaw's office was too small to examine all the town's people who had several of the same symptoms. Eugenist, along with Nurse Jeanita who had noticed the severity of Elphaba's condition by just looking at her, rushed down to town hall. Of all the cases of illnesses that Nurse Jeanita had helped diagnose the past two days, Elphaba needed immediate care. Some had come in complaining of nausea and headaches. Others complained of constant vomiting and diarrhea. Even others had a slight fever. With just a touch of Elphaba's forehead, Nurse Jeanita sensed her condition needed treatment. She was gravely ill. Nurse Jeanita pushed open the doors to the hall to let Eugenist carry his deathly looking sister in. Seeing Nurse Jeanita come rushing in after Eugenist, Doctor Shaw knew this patient needed his care urgently. Doctor Shaw had instructed Nurse Jeanita to stay at his office to try and treat any mild cases that came along and only send those who needed urgent attention. Standing up from the chair he sat in while treating a villager who complained of stomach pains, he rushed over to meet Eugenist. Of all the three hundred cases that Doctor Shaw had treated or was still treating, just glancing at Elphaba, hers appeared to be the worst. Doctor Shaw set up a cot away from all the other patients he was tending to. He instructed Eugenist to place her down carefully on the cot and asked Eugenist to step away for a moment while he examined her. Elphaba needed to be quarantined so as not to spread whatever she may be carrying. Doctor Shaw immediately started checking all her vital signs. Her blood pressure was extremely low and her fever was the highest he had ever seen recorded in all his years in the medical field. His concern for Elphaba showed clearly on his face. Even from the distance away Eugenist knew a serious situation had occurred within their village. Some sort of epidemic had taken place. As he looked around at all the other people within the hall no one looked as bad as his younger sister. Eugenist watched Doctor Shaw continue to work only on Elphaba, ignoring all his other patients. Eugenist sensed that her condition was by far the worst, a matter of life or death. This deeply troubled him. If anything were to happen to his sister he couldn't cope. Again, he was troubled just thinking about what he prayed wouldn't be the unimaginable outcome were she not to survive this crisis. Elphaba had to live. In fact Eugenist was so deeply troubled that he didn't know if he himself would ever be himself again.

◆

Helga had watched the chaos from across the street from Doctor Shaw's office. Townspeople were able to walk by themselves to the doctor's office. Helga would have bet her own life that villagers would have had to have been carried over. At least the ones that were alive anyway. Twice, she stopped fellow villagers to learn if there had been any casualties. None to date. Every person in the village feared for their own health. Rumors of some outbreak yet determined were set loose among them. Not a single person had died. And as she looked on, it seemed almost everyone was still breathing. Why and how no one in the village had succumbed to the poison truly baffled her. Rather it truly infuriated her. The dosage of the poison mixed in the cookie dough should have wiped out the whole town if even a fraction of an oatmeal cookie had been eaten. She was positive Eugenist would have used the mix. She had cast a spell on him to do just that. After all, many people were sick. Judging from what she could see, just not sick enough to die. Helga wanted to return to the quack doctor from whom she purchased the poison and demand her money back. She would in time. Right now she needed to concentrate on seeking some sort of revenge on her most hated town. While she was thinking her most evil thoughts so far, the only person who could help her destroy what was left of Duggandorf was Eugenist, and as she thought of him, he appeared in her view. He looked frantic. Helga watched as Eugenist carried his sister and even from Helga's distant view she noticed that she looked close to death. Then a new plan developed. Better still, she would ruin the life of the person who was supposed to finish off her ultimate plan. Helga would turn the town against the little man who did nothing but sneeze. And all at once it hit her. Just by his sneezing alone he would finish himself off. Helga left the spot where she stood watching all the sick people roam the center of town square. Tomorrow she would return to the hall that had been set up as a temporary clinic for all the sick villagers. Helga was certain Elphaba would still be there as she observed Eugenist running toward the hall with her and noting how limp her limbs were. The scene she would make would convince everyone just how all these people had been made ill. She would make sure that everyone from that day forward would be sick of Eugenist as well.

◆

As luck turned out, most everyone in the town of Duggandorf who had been ill, had been treated and while some still would have to remain in the shelter for the next couple of days, Doctor Shaw said it could have been a lot worse. Even Elphaba's condition in the last twenty-four hours was improving slightly. Her symptoms were indeed the worst of all the villagers. It would be a long healing process before Elphaba was out of the woods.

Almost every organ of Elphaba's had some damage from whatever it was that still puzzled Doctor Shaw. The tests he ran on all the sick people within Duggandorf came back negative. Not a trace of anything could be linked to a specific cause of the sudden illness that broke out among the villagers. Eugenist spent the night at her bedside praying the whole time for her recovery. This morning he sat by her side hoping she would awaken from whatever condition her body was trapped in. As Eugenist held his younger sister's hand he along with many other town's people looked toward the direction of the door. A loud, painful moan from the outside of the shelter seemed to be getting closer. Doctor Shaw motioned for Nurse Jeanita, who had stayed on in the sick ward to help, to let whomever was crying out in pain into the building. As Nurse Jeanita quickly opened the door she was immediately shocked at what she saw. Helga was being held by two townsmen by her arms and led in to see the doctor. Large crowds of villagers followed her path to the shelter and were squeezing into the hall to see what would happen next.

Helga's pitiful cries certainly got the attention of the town, which is exactly what she wanted, as she faked the loud outbursts. Helga slowly made her way over to the doctor, moaning and groaning the whole time. Then when she was certain she had everyone's full attention, she pointed over toward Eugenist. With her weakest and most timid voice she said, "Him. That man or should I say that tiny person of a man. He did this to me! No, he did this to all of us." People moved in closer to hear what she was saying gasping at what they thought they already did.

"Eugenist made us all sick! That day... I was in the store buying cookies... Yes, I believe it was Wednesday of last week..." Helga pretended to catch her breath. She had everyone listening as she accused Eugenist again, "He kept on sneezing into the bowl of dough that he carried away from me... after he served me some of those ..." Helga chose her next words carefully, "germ-infected cookies."

Everyone who had been staring at Helga now turned to face Eugenist with a glare in his or her eyes. Doctor Shaw, sensing turmoil begin to unfold, quickly asked, "Eugenist, Is that true? Would you have been so ignorant as to sneeze into the dough? I mean, I never even gave that any thought. But, it now makes sense."

Turning to the large crowd of villagers, both healthy and sick, the doctor questioned everyone, "How many of you here by a show of hands has eaten one or more of the Wibbles cookies in the last few days?"

None of the healthy villagers raised their hands but all of the infected people did. A loud roar of conversations was all going on at once. Doctor Shaw put up his both hands, "Please, let's not jump to conclusions. Let's think about this."

Eugenist let go of his sleep-induced sister and stood up making a plea he had no choice but to do, "I've never in all my years sneezed into any dough. I can't help my condition and you all know that. I always turn my head away and most of the time I put the bowl down and walk away. It never stopped you from coming into the store before. Please. believe me."

Helga spoke up first, "I was there and I saw you do it. And now look at me. Explain how everyone who ate your cookies is sick. Even your own sister that you almost killed. Couldn't you have sneezed somewhere else HACHEW?"

Confused, Eugenist said, "No... no... I don't remember. I CAN'T remember! Why are you doing this to me?"

Helga purposefully didn't call him by his name and deliberately emphasized on the word Hachew. Everyone gathered in the room started to ask him the same thing using the name Eugenist knew would now haunt him forever. Ashamed, embarrassed and mostly guilty for something he couldn't remember doing; Eugenist didn't know what to do.

The crowd of villagers, mostly his friends, were yelling for him to tell the truth. A truth he couldn't remember although he wished he could.

◆

Helga, still pretending to need assistance, let herself be guided over to an empty cot. She watched as Hachew squirmed in front of the large crowd. Helga ruined him. No one in their right mind would buy oatmeal cookies from the Wibbles. She was certain of that.

Helga wheezed as she was led over to the bed to be treated for symptoms that didn't exist. Everyone was so helpful. Even the doctor who never paid her any mind looked very concerned for her. Villagers were coming over to her and asking her if she would be okay. Duggandorf cared for her. After all these years they finally cared for her. Even if her plan had backfired, somehow something good had come of it. Now as Helga watched a humiliated Hachew make his way through the crowd and out into the streets, she knew that he would never again be accepted in the town of Duggandorf. She also knew that Hachew realized this too. As Helga placed her tired and weary head down onto the pillow to be examined, as many had watched, she whispered a haunting word that everyone was sure to remember, "Hachew, why did Hachew do this to ME?"

◆

Eugenist ran straight to the store and locked the door. Everywhere he ran, people stopped and pointed an accusing finger at him. In their eyes he would always be guilty. Even though deep down he knew he was innocent. And so for the next couple of hours and into the night Eugenist sat in the corner and collected his thoughts. His parent's had been notified about Elphaba's condition before the town had turned against him. Someone had ridden a horse to the town where they were and told them the news of their beloved daughter. They were expected back first thing tomorrow morning. Eugenist's next thought was of his loving younger sister and that if what they all said was true; he almost killed her with his germs. Elphaba meant the world to him and he was ashamed. Never again could he face his sister knowing that he had almost killed her. If only she hadn't eaten all those cookies. Now it made sense that she was the most sick of all the townspeople. No one would visit the Wibbles cookie factory again. His poppa and momma would be heartbroken. His father would not have anyone to whom he could pass the family tradition. Elphaba may never fully recover enough to work the long hours necessary by herself. The guilt was killing Eugenist. He knew his parents were well-off and would be able to make it without the income from the soon to be defunct store. He also knew he could never face his family again which hurt more than anything else. Just as he discovered what he would do next, the clock in the shop struck midnight. Eugenist had been bottled up inside the store the whole day. Not one customer came to the door foretelling a penniless future within Duggandorf. Quickly, Eugenist packed his few belongings and after writing a very long apology note asking for his family's and, especially his sister's forgiveness, he headed out the door and into the night. Eugenist knew he would never return and that hurt the most. He would always miss his baby sister and hoped she would miss him too. Eugenist would always be guilt-ridden by the fact that his germs almost killed her. What Eugenist didn't realize was that his sneezing into the dough that fateful day offset the poison with a positive chemical reaction. Scientifically, one that could never be explained. By his sneezing, magically all the innocent purities within his soul lessened the strength of the poison softening the deadly impact intended. That was the reason no one died. Poor Eugenist would never know or understand all that had happened as he hurried to leave forever and travel toward the direction of the Black Forest.

14

Emdee, Cranky, and the rest of the gang brushed themselves off after the last sneeze and started up the stairs to check on Hachew. He had been up there for quite a while, longer than the others had. When the six of them had finally made it to the landing they heard the start of a too familiar sound coming from the bedroom. No sooner a loud hachoo followed by the body of one of their own came sailing straight for them. Unprepared for the seventh dwarf, Hachew tumbled into them like a bowling ball hitting the pins. All six fell down as Hachew landed on top of the pack. The sneeze had blown Hachew out of his trance and into the others. Merry and Yourshyness stood up and helped Hachew to his feet.

Still somewhat shaken, Hachew thanked them for helping him up. Cranky now aware that trouble had somehow invaded their home, spoke first "I say we all get outta here and outta here fast! This is the doing of the evil woman we heard so much about. In fact, no woman is good as far as Ise is concerned."

Emdee grabbed Cranky by his suspender and pulled it back until it snapped on his back.

"Ouch, whatya do that for? Come on Emdee, let's get a goin!" Cranky said as he pulled on Emdee's hand leading him toward the steps.

Emdee pulled free of his grasp saying, "Now, wait just a section, second. Yeah, wait a second. Whatever this thing is, whether good or bad, it has us all in some sort of spell. One by two, I mean one, we have been transfixed in our own terrors. Don't ask me how I know you guys were terrified, I just blue,do. I just do. We all had some sort of purpose in reliving painful memories. All but Toodum that is. We need to let him rehash his past fears too."

A bunch of no's came from the group. Poor Toodum, so innocent and pure, stepped back into a corner. Together, the others were confused, feeling why should they let him relive a past that he too must have suffered in. The other five now stood in front of him as a shield, protecting their most beloved friend.

Annoyed at the others for not seeing it his way Emdee pleaded, "Can't you all see! This is something we have no control over. Some sort of puzzle that must be completed. We HAVE to let him go to his bed! Who knows, maybe that is where the person is! We have to and we have NO choice. I don't like it either, but I trust that it will solve our mystery. Now step aside so I can take him to the bed."

Emdee walked past the others who had now separated to clear a path. Emdee took Toodum, who was already shaking, by the hand and led him to his bed. Emdee stood there with Toodum as his heart was being torn inside out knowing he had to leave him. He turned around briskly to walk away. Toodum didn't move, as Emdee feared. Toodum just stood there knowing that he was next to suffer his long lost past. Toodum was childlike. So childlike that he looked like he had just seen a ghost. A ghost that truly petrified him.

Dolby Capers

Childlike little man, silenced from words that never come, So he shall be given the name of TOODUM....

-Osanna

15

Miles upon miles away in a vast land a simple munchkin infant was left at the doorsteps of a convent in the town of Slitherstone. Truly an eyesore in both appearance and height, Sister Patrice and Sister Mary Alice found him at the front doorsteps to the nun's convent that was attached to the only orphanage for the surrounding four towns and took him in. They had been returning from the orphanage after tucking all the children in for the evening when they heard a very weak small cry.

Knowing from years of experience what an infant's cry sounds like loud or not, they quickly spotted the child in a wooden bassinet on the top step. Alone in the dark and cold of the winter night, they picked up the very light bassinet and brought him indoors. The policy of the orphanage was that the sisters had to meet the mother or both parents that were giving their child up for adoption. If they deemed the situation could have no other outcome, then the child was turned over both legally and rightfully to the convent as the sole guardian of the infant. The nuns would raise the child as their own with funding from all the participating towns. If the child was adopted then it was for the benefit of the child's well-being to be part of a happy family. Most children had a better chance at being adopted as infants and up until the age of three or four. Couples who found it hard to have their own baby preferred to have an infant rather than an older child. After the age of four the chances of a child being placed in a loving home were slim. The child was and would be the legal responsibility of the sisters until they reached eighteen years of age when they would have to leave the orphanage to make room for the smaller ones. Combined, Sister Patrice and Sister Mary Alice had over seventy-five years in the orphanage and had never come across an abandoned infant like the one they found that night. Upon closer inspection of the nameless child they too were shocked at the funny looking expression the infant had on his face. He seemed so innocent yet for lack of a better choice of a word, dumb. He actually looked kind of mopey to the two sisters. Looking him over and making sure he had all his fingers and toes the two sisters came up with the name of Dolby. How they chose that name neither could explain. It just fit him. Looking like a goofy doughboy from the pastry mix they used, they took both words and put them together to form Dolby. Since he had no identification left with him from his heartless mother, they had every right to give him a name. Sister

Mary Alice, the taller and thinner nun with her gray hair and blue eyes, suggested Capers for his surname. Sister Patrice, the shorter plump nun with dark hair and brown eyes, while picking him up out of the bassinet, got tangled up with her cape. Dolby was so tiny that the black cape draped around him hung so loosely. Seeing the cape hanging, the word Capers popped into Sister Mary Alice's head and so the petite infant boy came to be known as Dolby Capers.

◆

Couples from the surrounding towns would visit the orphanage on a regular basis in hopes of fulfilling their desire for a family. Since Dolby was their newest addition to the brood of orphans, and perhaps the smallest in age and height, both sisters thought he would be adopted in a pinch. Unfortunately, couples would take one look at his unusual face and move on to the next available baby or child. This pattern continued from the early infancy and straight into his toddler years. Potential candidates, who were desperate and wanted nothing more other than a child of their own, all reacted the same when they saw funny-looking Dolby. Sister Mary Alice and Sister Patrice had thought they had heard every possible excuse as to why no one wanted poor Dolby. Each time the excuses got better letting both Sisters realize that Dolby's place would always be with them at the orphanage. Even as he continued to age and not grow in height his other faculties were stunted too. The nuns had taken him into the town of

Slitherstone to visit the doctor for a complete physical when they had first found him. The doctor gave them an answer they weren't prepared for. Dolby was and probably would always be a simple man. From what the doctor could diagnose and by measuring his bone structure it was his opinion Dolby would grow no taller than four feet ten inches and possibly might never speak. The nuns were horrified at the thought of Dolby remaining speechless. From what he could determine from his throat examination, the good doctor said he was born with very few vocal cords. Dolby could utter small sounds but that would be his maximum ability. Chances are that was why his parents gave him up on that dark, cold night. One look at the poor infant's face and its tiny body and the mother, father or both could never imagine having to raise such a simpleton. When the baby didn't cry like a normal baby should, it probably sealed the fate of the child from the moment of its delivery into this world.

So it was that each day would come and go and poor Dolby would always be overlooked while many other children left the orphanage to live in a family with loving parents. Dolby would always long for this to happen to him as well.

◆

As Dolby grew into a young boy, two good things were a result of his staying at the orphanage. Although he didn't speak and his features were odd, most of the other children liked to be around him. That was the first good thing about Dolby. Dolby was always happy and loved to have fun. He would entertain the younger children as well as the older ones by moving his body. The nuns along with the children found him quite amusing and laughed along with him. Sister Patrice and Sister Mary Alice had grown very fond of Dolby over the years and never permitted any child young or old to treat him any differently than they would be treated. If an incident took place where another child ridiculed Dolby, the nuns punished that child more severely to serve as a warning to the others not to even attempt the same behavior. During his schooling Dolby grasped and learned at a slower pace than the other children his age. His outward appearance may have looked rather simple but his intellect was a bit more advanced. The sisters only had to show him a question twice and he usually showed he understood faster than they had thought possible. Many times both Sister Patrice and Sister Mary Alice were baffled at his ability to pick up on a subject that sometimes the other children found more difficult. The doctor informed them years earlier that he would never be an above average student, but the sisters never gave up on him.

What the class did find humorous was as the smaller children in the orphanage grew; poor Dolby remained the same height. In class he sat high up on schoolbooks so as to see over his desk. Dolby found this amusing too, usually he pretended he was climbing a ladder to the top of a mountaintop rather than just to be at a level equal to the other children. As a reward for learning at an accelerated pace he was frequently rewarded with a treat the nuns had learned that he truly loved since he was an infant. Sister Mary Alice loved to make banana cream pie, which soon became a favorite for most of the children in the orphanage. She couldn't serve them fast enough when it came to Dolby. That was the second good thing the nuns discovered. When Dolby was treated to some banana cream pie for something good he may have done, he would eat the pie unaware of anyone or anything around him. For as long as it took him to finish his serving, which sometimes consisted of the whole pie, Dolby would be lost in a world all his own. Even now, as a young boy whenever he was given a piece of what everyone now knew was his favorite, Dolby would wander off to a spot by himself and sit down in a chair and eat his banana cream pie oblivious to who or what was around his surroundings. The sisters treasured the moments when they could watch him find such simple pleasure in consuming banana cream pie. This enjoyment which was so pure, that one-day in his very near future would almost destroy him.

◆

As a young boy, Dolby watched many of his close friends leave the orphanage with couples who had expressed interest in them. He was always elated when one of them was adopted. Others would be jealous and sulk for days on end but never Dolby who truly was the happiest for them. Like the proven statistics, older children had to possess a finer quality to stand out from the rest and catch the eyes of potential parents. There were some couples that wanted second children to add to their families and give their first adopted child a sibling. Usually as the baby they adopted got older, an older brother or sister served the purpose of completing them as a family.

Dolby was very fond of a little girl of about four or five that arrived and left the orphanage in just a few days. Dolby had never seen anyone or anything quite as beautiful as this little girl. Dolby had never gotten to know her name because she had left before he had the chance to be introduced. Dolby did remember how the little girl's fair complexion almost reminded him of a winter's glazing that covered the ground. Her hair was the darkest he had ever seen; almost as black as the night. When she smiled her whole face lit up like a Christmas tree. To Dolby, she was the fairest little girl he had ever laid eyes on. But as fast as she arrived, she was gone, saddening poor Dolby. What he didn't realize was that someday in the very distant future their paths would cross again.

◆

Dolby did stay away from one child in the orphanage who was anything but pleasant.

In fact most of the children young and old avoided her not so much because they wanted to, the girl herself preferred it that way. When they did attempt to befriend her, she purposely did something hurtful and even harmful to them. After one or two experiences were bestowed upon a sorry individual the message was clear enough for the others to stay far away from her. Both the nuns were conscious of her behavior and attitude toward the other children and watched her closely.

Dolby, being overly friendly to all the children learned the hard way. The girl was anything but pleasant in the orphanage and was constantly reprimanded for getting into mischief and trouble more than anyone else. Osanna hated the fact that she wasn't loved enough to be raised by her parents and had been given up for adoption. She, too, like Dolby was not attractive and she too watched many children find homes where they would be raised in a family. A family was what Osanna wanted more to be than anything else. So it was that her revenge was to make everyone in the orphanage pay for her misery. Although she hated her stay there, it was still the only place she could call home. Osanna was the same age as Dolby. She towered over him in height and had the longest, straight brown hair with deep-set brown eyes to match. Quite often she would push Dolby, since he was so small, out of her way to show him just who was the boss. Osanna was disgusted whenever she saw Dolby eating a banana cream pie and wanted nothing more than to shove one in his face. This kind of behavior went on for years making Osanna the only bad experience Dolby had to endure. Like all the others he eventually learned to keep his distance from her and rather, enjoy the company of all the other children who truly enjoyed his in return. He loved his stay in the orphanage and hoped to stay there even past his eighteenth birthday. The years continued to fly by and so after many years of ignoring her and keeping his distance the day had finally arrived. Within weeks both Dolby and Osanna would be turning eighteen. Sister Patrice and Sister Mary Alice made all the arrangements to send them on their way. A hefty allowance was given to the child to help them start their future endeavors. The nuns bought them some new clothes packing them along with their other clothing in a new suitcase donated by the church. For whatever reason that year the nuns made the only decision they had ever made differently. Sister Patrice and Sister Mary Alice decided to let Dolby stay on at the orphanage. He was so good with the younger child who looked up to him even if he wasn't considered too smart. Dolby and Osanna were called into the nun's office. They sat both Dolby and Osanna down together which they had always done with other children who were turning eighteen that year and sent them off together. Some would choose to live with one another while others went their separate ways. In this case, however only one was being sent off by herself. The nuns explained to both Dolby and Osanna their plans. Dolby would stay and Osanna, who the nuns were not sorry to see go, would leave by herself the day after tomorrow.

Dolby smiled, like the nun knew he would, with the prospect of staying on at the orphanage as a caretaker to the children. Both Sister Patrice and Sister Mary Alice were getting on in age and needed an extra hand around the building. Having Dolby, who was loved by all the children, stay enabled them to share their supervisory duties and concentrate more on finding the proper homes for the abundant amount of children who occupied the orphanage. Osanna, on the other hand, couldn't believe what she was hearing. As much as she despised the orphanage she still feared the outside world where she had never been. Sliverstone was a town big enough for a young girl to be afraid to live in. The nuns had given her no choice and she had to leave all by herself. Inside the orphanage the other children feared her, which delighted her. On the outside no one would fear her, which frightened her. Osanna was fuming with anger over the fact that a simple man like Dolby, who was a tiny mute, won the hearts of the nuns. She had to brave the new world alone while Dolby reaped all the benefits of a familiar home. Osanna didn't even thank the nuns for the many years spent with them. She stood up from the chair in the nun's office and turned away to make her final arrangements to leave the day after tomorrow to a place she didn't know. As Osanna walked past Dolby she glanced down at him as he sat there waiting to be excused. What a stupid fool he was, Osanna thought. Oh, how she truly hated him. Osanna was envious of him for being able to stay. So envious that she decided right then and there that if she ever had the opportunity to make him sorry, Osanna would see to that she did.

◆

Ten years had come and gone and Dolby stayed on helping the nuns, who were now very old, and still facing all the errands around the orphanage. The only thing Dolby didn't help them with was the teaching of the children because he was incapable. Never have spoken in his entire life made it impossible for him to teach the younger children. However, his mannerisms were expressed so diligently that his point always came across when he needed to instruct a young child with what to do. Dolby's favorite thing other than the banana cream pie that he still enjoyed as much as he did as a child was taking groups of children on nature walks through the surrounding woods of Sliverstone. Both nuns trusted him whole-heartedly with the children whether they were young or old. Hours upon hours he would take them on hikes making it a fun experience as he did. Upon returning, the children would share their adventures with both the nuns who were just as eager to listen to them. Becoming more adventurous, Dolby had taken them deeper and deeper into the woods. Taking the group that sometimes numbered in the teens or whether it was just a handful, Dolby treated every group with the same enthusasium as he explored new territories unknown to him with each new quest.

Dolby never took any chances with the welfare of the children and always looked out for their safety. Having fun was one thing, but endangering the life of a child was something he never could imagine. What Dolby didn't know was just how close he would come to imagining just that.

◆

The years were anything but kind to Osanna. She never made it further than a couple of miles away from the orphanage. She stayed in the big town of Sliverstone, which consisted of mostly farmland. Because of the close proximity to the orphanage, it made her feel somewhat safe. Finding work for someone not as pretty as she was even more difficult. Osanna traveled from farm to farm tending to chores most farmers wouldn't give to their own worst enemies. Osanna became weathered from years of outdoor hard labor. She looked like an old woman with her now scraggly long brown hair. She still stood tall even though she spent endless hours hunched over tending to the various animals and crops. After saving every penny she made and with no chance of ever walking down an aisle as a bride, Osanna bought a run-down cottage deep in the woods of Sliverstone. Far, far away from any people and real civilization. Osanna worked long hours in the heat of the hot sun in the summertime to the frigid air that blew across her face in the harsh winters. Rain or snow didn't keep Osanna from working in order to afford her meager existence which she had to endure daily in order to barely survive. Barely surviving was just what she was doing.

◆

Osanna was picking corn off the stalks. The fingers on her hand were sore from the many ears of corn that she broke off from the stalks in the field. Today was hotter than usual for this early in the summer and sweat had already formed on her forehead. Twice, she paused while picking to wipe the perspiration with the apron around her waist. Osanna lifted the apron and wiped her brows from the trickling sweat that dripped down her face.

As she was clearing the remainder off her face Osanna heard children laughing from far off in the distance. She tried to make out the several figures that walked together in a single line. She stopped what she was doing and made her way through the cornfield to the outside border of the hillside to get a closer look. Osanna arrived at the spot where she thought she heard the laughter. At least fifteen children pranced about singing and laughing through the woods of the nearby property. Even after all these years, Osanna still had no tolerance for children. But something was different about this group. The leader of the pack looked out of place as he tried to lead the group. He was wearing an oversized lime green tunic with a purple cap on his small head. The tunic hung loosely over his body. Then all at once it hit her. She recognized him immediately. He was the little man with whom she spent all those miserable years watching people adore only because he was simple. The tiny, stupid fool who became mesmerized just by eating banana cream pie. She could never forget his face. Underneath his purple cap was the baldest shiny head any one could ever have. Missing also was any facial hair. Dolby's face was baby smooth and even up until he was eighteen he had never had to shave unlike most boys who had reached puberty. Osanna ran along the cornstalks staying out of view until she was up ahead of them. Once she was at a safe distance she hid behind a large tree and waited until they passed. No one saw her as they swung their arms singing and laughing right along side of Dolby passing right next to where she hid. Osanna wanted to jump out and frighten the oh so innocent children. But she held herself back. Instead Osanna had a brilliant idea that just popped into her head. Over the next few days she would follow Dolby and his puppets as they pranced along the woods. She would seek her revenge against Dolby once and for all fulfilling the promise she had made to herself so many years ago. She would tell the farm owner that she was not feeling well before her shift was over and that she would need the next few days off. Either the farm owner would agree and grant her request or he would tell her not to report back at all. Whichever the case, Osanna couldn't care less about that at the given moment. What Osanna did care about was having Dolby pay the ultimate price for her injustice in life. An injustice that Dolby would pay for with his life.

◆

Days turned into weeks and weeks became months before Osanna finally had the opportunity to strike. She never did report back to work of her own accord. All the money in the world didn't matter as long as her plan could be put into effect. And today was the day. She had timed everything so perfectly. Osanna had watched Dolby's daily routine for what felt like an eternity. Every third time he went out for a hike with the children he marched in a different direction. In each direction he chose a different route trying not to duplicate their past outings. Dolby wanted each trip to be special for his group. The groups could be anywhere from two children to as many as twenty at a time. Osanna followed his pattern and hit it right. Dolby had left the orphanage with only two children this morning. Judging by their appearance the little boy and girl were no more than five years of age. Perfect for what she had planned. Osanna had made three banana cream pies fresh that morning. Knowing the path he would take if she routed it correctly from his past outings, Osanna ran around in circles making sure that the aroma of the banana cream pies lingered in his path. And sensing that some things never change she ran back deep into the woods to wait in her run down cottage for Dolby and his bratty little followers to arrive.

◆

Dolby loved the special trips he made with the children he so loved. Everyday he would take a different group of children out for a long hike into the woods if the weather permitted. Today was the day that little Josef and Molly were allowed to go along on his journey. Dolby took the path that led straight into the deep woods of the forest. Usually he liked to reserve those paths for when he had older children in the group. Josef and Molly had been so good these last few weeks and begged him to treat them to the scarier section of his hike. And at only five years old anything in the deeper forest would do just that. Dolby had hiked with his flapping arms and loose tunic swinging in the air while the two children followed along laughing. Then as if something had knocked the wind out of him, Dolby smelled the most irresistible, desirable smell. Dolby knew that aroma anywhere. It was his favorite dessert. The banana cream pie aroma was coming from everywhere. Dolby had to have it. He used all his senses trying to find where the smell was coming from and forgot everything else. Josef and Molly, now frightened by his strange behavior, fought desperately in trying to keep up. They kept him in sight the whole time afraid of the consequences of the woods if they didn't. Dolby zigzagged through the darkened woods from the shadows of the tall trees and forgot all about his little hikers. In a panic, Dolby started to run straight to where he thought the smell was coming from. It was just within his reach. From just over that hill hidden in the darkest part of the forest was a small worn-out looking cottage. Even from a great distance away, Dolby spotted the banana cream pie sitting on the windowsill and made a mad dash for his special treat. Little did he suspect that the only treat he would get was the trick behind it.

◆

From behind the curtain she had pulled to the side for a better view Osanna saw Dolby coming. She made her way over to the door but not before checking on the large fire she had started in the fireplace. Osanna had planned on cooking three more pies this afternoon. None of which would be flavored with bananas. These pies would consist of freshly burned humans.

◆

Dolby didn't even wait for someone to answer. He pushed open the unlocked door and walked right in. A woman who looked vaguely familiar stood off to his side smiling with the most horrific looking grin. Dolby stopped to examine her more closely when she suddenly took out a banana cram pie from behind her back and handed it to him. Dolby forgot where or when he had seen this woman and he didn't care. Dolby took the banana cream pie and sat in a chair she had pointed to over in the corner of the room on the opposite side of the hot burning fire. Osanna knew she was right all along about this silly little fool. She took the other two pies off the windowsill and placed them on the small snack table in front of him. Osanna knew she had plenty of time before she would have to deal with this imbecile. Right now she waited for the two innocent brats to appear. From where she stood Osanna had a clear view of them. Off in the distance, Josef and Molly held onto each other's hands as they made their way, frightened at what was happening, to the direction of her doorstep. Osanna tried to look like a nice woman only trying to offer them help. But from the eyes of two five-year olds she appeared to them as the ugliest witch they had ever seen.

◆

Josef and Molloy slowly and very cautiously stepped into the witches' den. As soon as they walked in they noticed Dolby sitting in the corner eating his banana cream pie that they too had smelled from afar. Immediately they called out to him for help, knowing even at the tender age of five that Dolby was useless while he was eating his favorite dessert. Dolby was in a world of his own, and Josef and Molly longed to be in it with him at that given moment instead of staring at this evil woman.

◆

Osanna walked ever so lightly on her feet as to not scare the little brats more than they were already. The heat from the fire was burning her back. Once she got behind them she would lock her front door and tie up the two annoying pests. Once they were securely fastened with the rope she had handy, she would do what she had dreamed of over these past few weeks. Osanna wanted nothing more than to burn the skin right off these two innocent little creatures.

◆

Osanna's plan had almost worked. After tightly securing the rope she had pushed the chairs with the children tied up back to back closer to the fire. Josef and Molly were crying hysterically and screaming from the burning heat coming from the fire. Molly's scream was ear-piercing for a little girl of five. Osanna looked around her small cottage for anything to use to shut her up. She spotted her apron hanging over her bedpost and went to grab it. Osanna would gag the girl to drown out her screams. In only a few more minutes she guessed it wouldn't matter either way but for the time being she wanted a little peace and quiet. Osanna laughed as she grabbed the apron. The idiot known as Dolby was quiet as a mouse. His back was to them so he was missing all the action though he would soon be a participant.

◆

Osanna moved ever so close to the nasty pests and had just placed her hands on their chairs. With one quick shove they would sail straight into the fire. As she bent over and was just about ready to push the chairs over, a loud crash sounded at her front door. The door itself flew off the hinges and landed a few inches from her feet. Startled, Osanna stood straight up and was shocked to see two woodsman enter her home. The taller and better looking of the two grabbed her by both arms and pulled them behind her back holding her in place. The shorter woodsman ran to the children and untied them. Both Josef and Molly jumped up and together smothered the man with hugs who had now saved their lives. Recognizing Dolby, the good-looking one spoke first, "Are you crazy, you old fool. If we didn't happen to be passing by and hear those deafening screams, God only knows what you were going to do." He pulled on her arms more tightly and continued, "What in the name of God were you going to do? You will pay for this my dear friend. And severely I might add. I am Wince Charming, soon to be prince of this region of woods, and I demand you to answer!"

Knowing full well that she had lost and would now pay the ultimate price, Osanna tried to bargain with the soon to be woodsman prince, "Please, can't you see… It wasn't me…It was that little fool of a man…" Pointing over at Dolby, Osanna kept repeating, "It was him. All along he made me do this. Ever since we were children I wanted to do this.

I wanted to get revenge on the little troll…Please… You must believe me… It was TOODUM!" Confused by what she just called him and realizing it all made sense in describing the little man she would always know as Toodum, she laughed, "Toodum, that's it. It was Toodum. Such a stupid little man. Such an idiot. Toodum! Toodum! Toodum!" Toodum were the last three words she said, as the future handsome prince whisked her away from her cottage. Osanna was leaving the last place she would ever know as home.

◆

Dolby was upset, confused and even baffled as he was led to the front door of the only place he had ever known as home. Sister Patrice and Sister Mary Alice, both with tears in their eyes, had no other choice. Dolby was a danger to the children of the orphanage and could never be trusted with their safety again. He endangered the lives of Josef and Molly and if not for the devotion of the now old nuns of Sliverstone, chargers would have been pressed on poor Dolby. Both nuns pleaded in his defense and because of their life-long commitments to the children of the orphanage, Dolby was spared. The only sacrifice that had to be made was that Dolby would have to leave the orphanage as well as the town of Sliverstone. The nuns begged that he was just a simpleton, but that town council didn't care anymore. The safety of all the children had to be considered and having Dolby around wouldn't be wise. So as Sister Patrice and Sister Mary Alice carried his suitcase along with most of their life savings that they gave to him, they tried in vain to comfort the truly frightened Dolby. Both of the sisters blamed themselves for his misfortune. They should have known that someone as evil as Osanna would one day return to do the unthinkable. But it was too late and Dolby was fooled into not doing a thing to help the children and now he must pay the price. The nuns had waited until the clock struck midnight before they ushered him off into the night. All the children, including Josef and Molly who had since forgiven him, would be beside themselves with grief when they woke up tomorrow morning realizing Dolby was gone for good. They still to this day loved him and enjoyed being around him. But the decision was made and the nuns had to act fast. The council had given them enough time and twice they had missed the deadline. Sister Patrice and Sister Mary Alice planned his departure carefully as to not have the children see him leave. They both hugged him goodbye with tears streaming down their faces. It was too painful for both of them. He had been a part of them for so many years and now he was leaving. Sister Patrice handed his suitcase and a basket along with enough food to last him at least a month. Sister Mary Alice took his other hand and placed a map with a path for him to follow. Dolby cried silent tears as he walked away from the only two people he ever knew truly loved him. The children did too but not like the nuns. The door closed behind him, leaving Dolby all alone in the darkness. Frightened and scared, Dolby opened the map and with his keen sense of direction headed straight toward the Black Forest.

16

Unlike the others, Toodum had snapped out of his trance of his own free will. Standing in front of his bed Toodum refused to move and was now even smiling. Toodum thought back to the time when he first encountered his six now life-long friends. He had been traveling through the Black Forest for the rest of the night and most of the next day. For some strange reason and even until this day, Toodum had the familiar tune of Heigh-Ho embedded in his brain. With any thought to the song, he automatically felt the need to whistle, even if it took all of his effort to barely do so.

Emdee, Cranky and the others also shared the same feelings whenever they tried to remember just how the tune Heigh-Ho came to be inside their heads. The result was always the same. None of them could figure out precisely how the song was put into their heads or better still entered into their minds. Yourshyness said it was as soon as he entered the Black Forest that the tune kept on repeating itself over and over until he let it in to his head. Dozzey, Hachew and the others all agreed it was the same way for them too. How could a song or tune be placed inside someone's head without them agreeing or disagreeing? One of life's still unanswered questions among the seven of them. As if it were only yesterday, Toodum remembered approaching the diamond mine entrance. The glistening jewels were shining more than ever since the sun was so close to setting. The gleam off the diamonds reflected in Toodum's eyes and led him straight toward the opening. And from seven different directions, each of them all wound up at the diamond mine at the same exact time. Some were confused; others angry, and perhaps one or more were relieved to come upon six individuals much like themselves. All of them were the same or close to one another in height. Each of the seven had never come across another human being such as themselves and together they were all stunned to be looking each other up and down. If memory served Toodum correctly, it was Emdee who took the leadership position from the start. Huddled now inside the mine, Emdee went around the group asking for introductions. Ironically, none of them gave their birth names. Each one of them chose to use the name that would fit their experience to a tee. An experience none of them would ever share in public. And so it began, that seven somewhat identical small men began a life as one. They set up shelter in the mine and later on built their wooden cottage with all its fine amenities. As for their life's work they chose to work inside the diamond mines and save their diamonds for a rainy day. A rainy day that had never come until Toodum broke free from his memory to see an object under the sheets of his bed.

17

The object in the sheet started to rise. From where Toodum stood, the sheet rose like a ghost that flies through the air around cemeteries. Emdee, Cranky and the others, who all had been carefully monitoring Toodum to ensure his safety, slowly made their way over to him. They were all linked together holding one another's hand as they approached Toodum, who had now stepped back from his bed to watch the rising spirit.

The sheet grew taller and taller as it rose to stand on the bed. No one knew what to do or even had the nerve to speak up to confront the object. They continued to stare in disbelief at the scene unfolding in front of them. Suddenly the sheet slid to one side of the creature underneath it. Relieved it wasn't a spirit or ghost, but still unsure of what it actually was, the group stood firm. The creature started to move from side to side to free itself of the now tangled sheet wrapped around it. After what felt like hours but was only a matter of a few seconds or a minute at most, the creature had finally come free of its entanglement. All seven of the now life-long friends stood there with their eyes wide open and their mouths too. No longer frightened, the seven little men, each had a different angle and view of the beautiful young girl who faced them all. Still silent, they all watched as the fairest maiden they had ever laid eyes on stretched from the long nap she had taken. So long that seven terrifying pasts had been relived by each of the group in flashbacks within their minds. With hair as dark as the night and a complexion as light as a winter's dusting, she was indeed the most fairest of them all. Toodum, especially, seemed most pleased by her presence. Having once seen a little girl from years ago come and go within a blink of an eye from the orphanage, Toodum wondered if this maiden could be her. Being speechless he could never ask and only hoped that if she ever did talk of her past, and heard the mention of a Sister Patrice or Sister Mary Alice then certainly it was she. Delighted with that prospect, Toodum started to spin in circles as his tunic flapped lazily around him. The fairest maiden stepped off the bed and now stood smiling in front of each one of the seven little men. Emdee, Cranky, Dozzey, Merry, Yourshyness, Hachew and Toodum, who had since stopped spinning, were all in a single line. With the most soothing and peaceful voice, the fair maiden then pointed to each of them and from memory of the names she came across on their bed frames, called each by name. Surprised at how she just did that, without knowing anything about them, the seven, still quiet, smiled in return. The fair maiden looking at all their silly expressions, that she knew she would love forever, started to laugh. Her beauty and the calmness that she radiated had all seven little men laughing right along. Together, the eight of them would share what others longed for. A life of love, health and happiness. And as a newly formed group they would all live happily ever after. Or so they thought...

18

High atop the mountain and overlooking the entire region of several dozen towns and the Black Forest was the darkest, dreariest castle. A lingering black cloud circled over the castle with bolts of lightning that periodically flashed overhead. Within the cinderblock walls was the most evil Queen who had ever lived. The Queen lived alone except for the company of her beloved black crow. Years of loneliness didn't bother her. She longed for the solitude of her empty castle. Others would never survive living as secluded as she.

The Queen enjoyed isolation from civilization. The large mirror that hung in the main hall leading to the vast rooms throughout the castle was her other companion. Spells, magic and witchcraft were child's play to the powers that she had accumulated over her lifetime. Powers that she used to win over the heart of the now deceased King who once resided in this long ago vibrant castle. Dark and dismal replaced the bright and lively interior that once filled the whole castle and the surrounding grounds. Hillsides and pastures were plentiful and green. Wildlife roamed the grounds being nourished off the land. But all that too had changed. With limited sunshine, the greener pastures had since turned brown and the animals that once grazed, left for other regions with better possibilities for nourishment. The Queen couldn't care less. Her sole existence was to be the fairest of them all. Day after day and week after week, the Queen would look into her magical mirror and ask for the one response she had always dreamed of. Each time the answer would be the same. There was a young maiden that was the fairest of them all and would be for as long as she walked the face of earth. After year upon year of trying in vain to track down this obstacle rather than competition, her efforts were feeble. Somehow, someway, and even someone had always seemed to protect this maiden from the wrath she had wanted to inflict upon her. So as the Queen stood in front of this magical Mirror, she looked at her reflection. A reflection she hated. At six foot two and a long slim build, she barely fit within the mirror's frame. Wearing her long black cape with the attached black hood covered her short black hair that she never exposed. While her face disturbed her most, her pointy ears which over the years people ridiculed caused her much pain. Her bird-beak nose and long pointy chin along with her dull brown eyes completed the picture. A picture she would have ripped up if she ever got the chance. All the spells and magic couldn't change her appearance as long as the fair maiden lived. Tracking the maiden down was her burden for most of her life. Once the King had died from his sudden illness, which most thought it was, but the evil Queen knew better, the staff within the castle was immediately fired and her mission began. Her mission to find the fair maiden and put her out of commission for all of eternity.

19

From as early as the evil Queen could remember after her so-called beloved's passing, she used every spell and piece of magic imaginable to find the whereabouts of this maiden who stood in her way of her attaining ultimate and ever-lasting beauty. She wanted to be simply irresistible and with the young maiden alive this was impossible.

So, from the moment of the young maiden's birth, she cast every spell possible to find the girl. From looking in her magic mirror she was able to see every town within the region.

Year upon year the result was the same and no sign of the maiden turned up.

The evil Queen had to devise her most powerful plan to date.

She needed to form an unknowing group to lead her to the maiden. The maiden who would eventually stumble upon them first deep within the woods of the

Black Forest. What she came across in each village sealed her plan of action. In seven different towns were seven little men and each possessed a quality she could use to overcome her constant struggle to find this fair maiden. Unbeknownst to the seven little men, they would be linked together forever. The evil Queen would see to that and studied them closely during their early years. Seven individuals with seven different personality traits but one common factor. They were all much shorter than the average person. Some townsfolk overlooked it, others despised it, and even others embraced their appearance. Using her powers she had cast a spell on seven other individuals within each of their seven villages. These unsuspecting people played very important roles in shaping the future of each little man, and a future where she could destroy the one person who blocked her path, her road to being beautiful.

20

So as the evil Queen pulled the strings on her innocent puppets, they all behaved in the manner she had planned for them. Recalling their names in order, the Queen laughed to herself. Hiltrude, Esperanza, Inga, Gaston, Hanna, Helga, and even Osanna led despicable lives. They had been chosen because she knew she could help control, and if not, then at least see to it that their destiny would be anything but good. As she hoped, she succeeded in helping to destroy each one of her clueless helpers. In return her unknowing puppets helped to destroy each of the seven little men. The personality traits became their beings and their beings became almost nothing as each one of the seven little men fled from their beloved villages because of circumstances she had orchestrated. Fearful, hated, banished, ashamed, embarrassed, guilt-ridden and never fully understanding what had taken over their once peaceful lives forcing them to head directly toward the Black Forest.

Planting the final seed, the evil Queen had cast a spell which made each little man hear a familiar sound that would cause them to whistle the tune wherever they went after first entering the Black Forest. Each little man would not know how the tune came to be, but none of them would question why they shouldn't whistle it. The Queen programmed them so she could know their whereabouts at all times. Using the first initial from each of her unknowing puppets' names, she came up with HEIGH-HO. This was her most original spell ever. "Heigh-ho, heigh-ho, it's off to work we go," and to work they always would. It was a sure way for her to track the seven little men since the melody had become part of their daily lives. A day would never go by where they wouldn't whistle that tune and she would know where they were. However, something was still not right. The Queen knew her final plan needed something more. After watching each little man develop his own defining personality trait, she realized what was missing. The Queen craved her own personality trait which was to be the eternal beauty of the entire world. The fair maiden now had that distinction and she wanted it. Not until that very moment did she realize just how she would get it. She, herself, would have to obtain the outer beauty by doing what she knew she had to do. The Queen would follow the whistles to the cottage where she knew the fair maiden would be. How she knew, she didn't quite understand herself. For the first time in her life not even her powers or any other magic could tell her how she knew of the whereabouts of the maiden.

The Queen just did. So when the seven little men left for their daily work down at the mine, she would pose as an old, shriveled hag and offer the fair maiden eternal youth.

Perhaps something with poison. After the maiden ate it and fell into eternal rest, she could be the fairest of them all. Or so SHE thought. Either way someone would live happily ever after. With all of her plotting, scheming and planning, the Evil Queen was convinced she would prevail. Or would she? ……………………..

About the Author

This is a fourth novel for Vincent N. Scialo. Unlike his previous three novels, this is his first attempt at a dark fabled fairytale. Set in old Victorian times with the names of his characters to reflect the era, Vincent promises that you will once again be in for the ride of your life. Each character will embrace you and win you over right from the start. Letting them go will be harder than you imagined, with their images staying inside your head for endless days.

His first novel *The Rocking Chair* has received much acclaim since its publication three years ago. The sequel *Randolph's Tale (A Journey for Love)* seems to hold the promise of another success!

For those who love suspense thrillers, *Deep in the Woods*, will be sure to please.

This is a novel that will keep you up late at night with the lights on.

Vincent continues to perfect his work while residing in Bellmore, Long Island, with his wife Jennifer and their two children.